FOR BOOKS' SAKE AND LONDON ROLLERGIRLS
PRESENT

Derby
Shorts

THE BEST NEW FICTION FROM THE ROLLER DERBY TRACK

For Books' Sake and London Rollergirls present
**DERBY SHORTS**
The best new fiction from the roller derby track

www.forbookssake.net
www.londonrollergirls.com


This first edition published by Group Of in 2013

© Group Of 2013

All texts © 2013 by the authors

Group Of
www.groupof.co.uk

Edited by Jane Bradley

Designed by Group Of

ISBN 978-0-9566651-1-9

A catalogue record for this book is available from the British Library

# CONTENTS

# INTRODUCTION

"Where's the ball?" "Do you beat each other up?" "How do you score points?" "Do you all wear fishnets?"

So many questions.

If you are unfamiliar with the sport of roller derby, read on...

Roller derby is a full contact sport played on quad skates. A roller derby game (known as a "bout") consists of two teams of four defensive players and one jammer – the point scorer. The game begins with the pivots and the blockers (defensive players) skating in front in a tight formation (the pack).

The jammers race to pass through the pack once, at which time no points are scored – but a "lead jammer" position can be established. They continue to race around the track a second time and attempt to pass the pack again. The jammers score one point for each opponent they lap as long as they pass that player in bounds and without penalties.

The jammers may continue to race and score points for two minutes or until the lead jammer "calls off the jam" (by tapping her hands on her hips). Generally, a jammer scores four points each time she makes it through the pack within bounds and five points if she laps the other jammer.

Like any sport, roller derby has many detailed rules – including no fighting, tripping or elbowing – but, obviously, the team with the most points at the end of the game wins!

(And, no, there's no ball.)

During the six years I have been a member of London Rollergirls I have lost count of the number of times I have been asked by friends, family and colleagues the questions above. However, the most common question is simply "why?"

Why do rollergirls devote so much of our time to skating? Why do we spend several evenings a week trekking to various far-flung parts of our cities for training? Why do we spend countless hours a week at committee meetings and off-skates training sessions? Why do we abandon other social commitments and forget our non-skating friends in favour of discussing the minutiae of rules and strategy and watching bout footage with our teammates?

It is answering the whys that is the hardest. Replying with "because I love it" just isn't enough. The truth is, roller derby is not just a hobby and definitely far more than just a fun way to get fit.

By celebrating the writing talent of the roller derby community in this anthology we hope to share the passion, the love and the dedication we – and that includes skaters, referees, non-skating officials, fans and jeerleaders – all have for this sport. We are a diverse bunch of people from different backgrounds, careers and social circles; but we come together in sports halls, rinks and on tracks across the globe, united in our love for roller derby.

We want to answer the "whys" by capturing the heart and soul of this ever-changing game on its inexorable rise, from its DIY ethos and punk-rock roots, to the strength and athleticism on display at bouts all over the world. The sport has grown dramatically since the early 2000s, when the Texas Rollergirls began the modern revival of women's flat-track roller derby, and there are now over 1,200 (and counting!) leagues worldwide. It truly is an exciting time for roller derby and London Rollergirls are thrilled to work with For Books' Sake on this anthology to offer a glimpse into the heart of our community.

Welcome to our derby family!

*Helen Nash, London Rollergirls*

# FOREWORD

We love roller derby. We really do. You might say we're obsessed. Fanatical, even. And London Rollergirls were the first roller derby league we ever saw bouting live, so they've long held a special place in our hearts. London Rollergirls were our first derby love, so when we got the chance to collaborate with on this anthology, we were beyond excited.

There's a lot of things we love about roller derby. The athleticism, the adrenaline, the euphoria and the excitement. It's sport, subculture and community all rolled into one. It's a world where fierce, powerful women are idolised for their strength, strategy and stamina, but that at the same time champions and celebrates everyone involved. And with over a thousand leagues and countless more fanatics and followers all over all the world, it's become a family and a home.

It has its fair share of exhaustion, bruises and heartbreak, but that just makes us love it all the more. Because it's life in microcosm; no-one escapes without collateral damage like cuts, grazes and the odd broken bone. And every extended family has its factions, frustrations and occasional in-fights. But we love it despite and because of these things, for all of these reasons and so many more.

And that's why we're so happy and proud about the collection we've compiled in *Derby Shorts*. The short stories showcased in this anthology reflect the range of roller derby; the inevitable rivalries, anxiety and insecurities, but also the solidarity, drive and energy behind every bout.

So what are you waiting for? Get those skates on and get stuck in.

The pack is here.

## THIS IS NOT YOUR GREAT-GREAT-GREAT GRANDDAUGHTER'S DERBY

**Kaite Welsh**

It starts by accident. Emily Featherstone is the first – Emily Featherstone is always the first to master any new fashion, the rest of us just follow in her well-shod footsteps – and she arrives at one of our mother's At Homes wielding a pair of the strangest shoes any of us have ever seen.

"It's the latest thing," she insists, and we nod along, not entirely sure if this is just another one of the 'entertaining' practical jokes with which she livens up the Season. Last year, she dressed her scullery maid up in her brother's suits and sent her courting Caroline Leigh. It went on for months, until the maid tired of the charade, handed in her notice and moved to Caroline's household. The whole experience must have scarred Caroline, because since then she seems to have completely abandoned her search for a husband.

But Emily actually carries through with her plan of wearing the rolling skates out in public, and we watch in jealous fascination as she takes her first wobbly turn around the bandstand in Regent's Park, secretly hoping that she'll lose control and end up in the Serpentine.

"It's glorious," she pants, as she collapses onto the grass (much to the horror of our chaperone, who had covered her eyes during the entire display). "Theodora, try it!" Dora does so obediently whilst her twin sister Thomasina looks on, practically green with envy. We each take turns until the late afternoon light fades into evening, the sinking sun setting the rose garden ablaze.

Over dinner, I announce that I want – no, I need – my own pair of rolling skates.

I can read their answer in their expressions. Clumsy Diana, who can barely walk in a straight line without falling over, who came perilously close to wobbling as she curtseyed to the Queen during her debut, who dances like she has lead in her shoes – that girl on wheels?

"Never," my father replies firmly.

"But Emily Featherstone says it's the very latest thing," I try. Emily is their ideal of what a daughter should be – pretty, graceful, a witty conversationalist. It bemuses them that this is her second Season, another attempt at finding a husband. I can only assume that any potential suitors have been frightened off by her implacable perfection, which is cold comfort when she's the toast of every ball and my dance card is perpetually half-empty.

Over the next few weeks, girl after girl shyly shows off her latest acquisition. Bored horses lounge in stables, their riders otherwise occupied. Drawing masters complain of inattention, or that their students only want to draw women in motion, gliding through the parks on wheeled shoes. Mothers tut over their tea and scones that this new fad is gauche, unladylike, and bound to lead to injury. Their fears are confirmed when Violet Fitzherbert breaks her ankle, even though she had been showing off – skating backwards into a passing cyclist, and nobody was confiscating his bicycle – and we'd all warned her not to anyway.

Still, they don't stop us, and for a few blissful stolen hours a week, we swoop around Regent's Park in slow, graceful glides.

At first.

It starts subtly, with Caroline trying to outpace Emily. Then Thomasina claims she stumbles, knocking Theodora flying with her bustle. Parasols are outlawed after an incident involving Margaret Smythe's ferrule, Veronica Roberts' eye and a mysterious lack of witnesses. Since this was the month after Veronica had stolen Margaret's fiancé, it was quietly felt that she had gotten her just desserts and that in any case there would be plenty of time before the wedding for that bruise to heal.

Over tea and cake, girl after girl brags that her mother is on the verge of forbidding her from skating, after she came home with muddied skirts and torn stockings. Or that the scrape along her jawbone where she met the ground face-first has left her confined to the house for a week because she can't possibly go to Mrs Astley's dinner party looking like a common ruffian. They tell their stories with glowing pride, as well as the occasional glimmer of relief. Mrs Astley's dinner parties are universally acknowledged to be dire.

Still, we silently agree to the charade that these incidents are accidental, refusing to publicly countenance the idea that we deliberately wish harm on our dearest friends. Even when Thomasina and Theodora collide near the Serpentine after a morning of sniping that one of them borrowed the other's hat without permission, they dust themselves off, their apologies profuse if conspicuously lacking in sincerity.

Somehow, our little group of well-bred gentlewomen splits into two factions. Those of us who have been secretly chafing under Emily's yoke for some time now take great pleasure in being able to skate faster than our Queen Bee and her pretty drones. They in turn reveal that their ability to land a stinging verbal blow is matched by their ability to jostle one with an elbow, or accidentally knock us down during a supposedly friendly circuit of the Park. Soon, the cracks in our polite facade spread in a spiderweb of rivalry. Petty jealousies bubble to the surface and old wounds are reopened.

The truth is, we have always been competing against one another. To be prettier, more accomplished, better-dressed. To be the most marriageable. And though none of us dare say it, this new contest is so much more fun.

Beneath hooped skirts and puffed sleeves, we discover muscle and sinew. Our mothers might tut if the pianoforte's ruffles slip, exposing a curved wooden leg, but in secret we lift our petticoats and compare calves and thighs. We have little care anymore for how shapely our ankles are, or how we match up against our friends. For once, spindly little Melanie Waltham finds that her size works in her favour – light on her feet, she's faster than any of us. Margaret Smythe, long the butt of jokes for her less than fragile form, discovers that she is a formidable opponent when it comes to blocking rival skaters' paths.

With the competition openly acknowledged, our late-afternoon circuits of the Park become more structured. The race is always between two girls, their friends following in packs, jostling each other and fighting to help their leader forward – or tug their rival back. It's easy to hide in the pack at first, one more corseted body jabbing and shoving. The bravest among us kick, lifting one foot up daringly and aiming it squarely at someone's ankle. I stumble home black and blue, and try to hide my wincing when Arthur Pendleton, a friend of my brother's, asks to take me for a turn around the garden.

To my surprise, he is enthralled by my new pastime.

"You're one of those skating girls, aren't you?" he asks in a low voice, as though he doesn't want anyone to overhear us. A thrill shivers through me. "I must say, it's terribly brave. I've seen how fast you all go – you're positively fearless!" The fact that he has been watching us – watching me – should make me feel self-conscious. Instead, I feel the way he describes me. Fearless.

Arthur isn't the only one to notice me.

"Diana Goddard," Caroline calls one afternoon as we're practising falling with a modicum of grace. "You've got decent speed. Let's see you in front."

I inch through the gathered group of girls, feeling every pair of eyes on me. My legs feel wobbly and for once it has nothing to do with the wheels strapped to my feet. Being part of something, a gang of sorts, is one thing. Being singled out is quite another. As I take my place at the front of the assembling pack, I hear my mother's litany of instructions in my head. A lady doesn't put herself forward. A lady doesn't run. A lady never, under any circumstances, draws attention to herself.

When I push off, propelling myself across the curving path away from the others, I feel as though I've left Mother's rules on the ground behind me and all I want is to get away, away from the lectures and the dress fittings and the tutting of relatives when I stumble over a passage on a piano I never wanted to learn to play anyway. I feel like I'm flying and I never, ever want to touch the ground.

It's then that Margaret thuds into me from behind and we both go sprawling on the grass.

When Caroline skates smoothly over, her forehead wrinkled in a frown, we're doubled up, laughing like hyenas, in a tangle of skirts and legs and skates.

"Not bad, Goddard," she says grudgingly. "Next time, watch your back." She compliments Margaret on a particularly effective block, although I would prefer the term 'common assault,' and glides off leaving us both speechless with delight.

As the weeks go by, we skate faster and push harder. The resulting injuries escalate, and our tense friendly rivalry threatens to spill over into all-out war.

It all comes to a head at Amanda Trefusis' younger sister's debutante ball. Whispers fly around the ballroom that our presence is required in the library immediately on a matter of great importance. I can't help but be secretly relieved to leave the scornful gaze of younger girls enjoying their first Season, who consider us old maids already.

Emily and Caroline sit in armchairs that look like thrones. Though they will barely look at one another, it is clear they are co-conspirators.

Caroline clears her throat, but Emily speaks first.

"It's clear that there have been some... incidents of late," she says diplomatically.

Amanda snorts. "Incidents? Gertrude Middleton has a cracked rib!"

"Gertie laces her corsets too tight," Emily says with a dismissive wave of her hand. "It was only a matter of time before she did herself an injury. If she really thinks anyone believes she comes by that eighteen-inch waist honestly with the amount of scones she put away the other week – "

"The point is," Caroline interrupts, "is that we need some rules. Honestly, my brother's rugger injuries look like child's play compared to some of the accidents we've had."

"The point is," Emily cuts in, "that they aren't accidents. Now we're not advocating that we give up the roughhousing completely. I think," she adds with a wicked smile, "that we're all finding it most... stimulating."

"I haven't had this much fun since Harry Wyndham asked me to waltz with him at my coming out ball," Violet sighs.

Caroline frowns. "Didn't he walk away with a broken wrist?"

"He was a little over-familiar. Not a mistake I believe he'll be making again." Violet looks positively smug.

It seems that we've been carrying around seeds of violence and anarchy for years. It just took a pair of skates to let them grow. It takes the best part of the night, but we establish a set of rules to limit the damage. War wounds are all very well, but no one wants to cripple themselves and risk permanently being banned from taking part.

Among other things, it is clear that more practical clothing is required if our maids and dressmakers have anything to do with it. We agree a basic uniform of thick skirts and loosened stays, and Caroline takes to wearing navy blue worsted stockings to skate in – in honour, she says, of our bluestocking intellectual foremothers. She looks a fright, but somehow we all follow suit and the nickname sticks. It becomes traditional that whoever is leading the Bluestockings in a race wears a blue ribbon in her hair to distinguish herself from the others, and soon we find ourselves wearing them to all sorts of occasions as a badge of honour. Within weeks, you can tell a Bluestocking from a Currer Belle – the name Emily christened her team in response, after the pseudonym Charlotte Brontë adopted when she took on her own unfeminine endeavour – regardless of whether or not they're on skates.

And then a strange thing happens.

One day, whilst paying calls with Mother, the younger daughter of a family friend shyly reveals to me a bracelet of blue ribbon.

"We watch you all the time," she whispers excitedly, explaining that she and her governess are Bluestockings admirers. "I'm dying for a pair of rolling skates," she sighs. "Mother has promised that if I master Beethoven's sonatas by the time I'm ready to be presented at court, she'll buy me a pair. Do you think Caroline might let me skate with you?"

When I recount this in a hushed voice over the dinner table to Violet, she has a story to match. Soon enough, the only topic on the lips of the London debutante is whether or not one is a follower of the Bluestockings or the Currer Belles. Friendships end and engagements are called off over it – even our mamas find themselves at odds with one another if their daughters are in opposing teams.

One day Emily storms into my mother's At Home, eyes blazing, barely waiting to be announced. The butler's an ardent Blue anyway, and I can tell from his expression that he wouldn't have expected better from the leader of the Belles.

"Those jumped-up little minxes," she seethes. "Have you heard? A new league's been formed in Bath. The Northanger Abbesses. They claim they're faster than either of us."

"Well I for one won't stand for it," Thomasina announces stoutly.

"Nor I," her twin, for once in agreement, adds.

The Bluestockings and Currer Belles are now united in two things – our love of rollerskating and the conviction that the Northanger Abbesses are in dire need of a harsh lesson.

"I'll write to them," Emily announces. "See if they have the courage to come up against us in person."

"We'll both write to them," Caroline amends. "A friendly – but firm – letter from the founders of the sport, kindly inviting them to watch how it should be done."

Soon enough the Abbesses are descending on their London relatives, skates in their suitcases.

Although it's irrational, I feel protective of our hobby. I don't want to meet these other girls who think that they can compete with us, I don't want to be judged and found wanting in the only area of my life that I am truly confident.

My fears are unfounded. The Northanger Abbesses, as they squeeze into Emily's parlour, look perfectly normal. They are stout, skinny, short and gangly. Some of them are pretty, some are plain. And they all look as nervous as we are.

"Your park looks simply marvellous," one of them starts awkwardly. "But how on earth do you manage not to fall in the river?"

Hours go by as we talk – comparing tricks to go faster or trip up one's opponent, and discussing the best way to bribe a lady's maid not to breathe a word of the bruises, grazes and muddy petticoats.

They're not our rivals, I realise. They're just like us. Women who were bored, restless, full of an energy they couldn't name much less exercise. Girls who talked about the weather over tea or the latest fashions over a glass of lemonade at a ball, confined to dance steps and sitting prettily when they wanted to run and shout.

Some of us gather together for a game of tennis, and for the first time I find myself not holding back. Gone are the polite little taps of racquet against ball – I swing it like a croquet mallet above my head, brandish it like a weapon. It's the first tennis match I've ever won, and I'm flushed with success as we go indoors, where I walk straight into Arthur Pendleton.

"Gosh," he says as we right ourselves, blushing, "you look like you've been braving the elements, not playing tennis!"

The other girls are amused, but Mother is horrified and pushes me up the stairs to change and arrange my hair. I'm the picture of prim perfection when I enter the dining room for luncheon, but something in Arthur's eyes suggests he isn't fooled for an instant.

Conscious of Mother's disapproving gaze, I nibble on cold chicken delicately. But when she is distracted, Arthur slips me some of his in a napkin, and it's in that moment I decide I love him.

Our antics have been gathering an audience for weeks now – where once people just so happened to be walking in the Park whilst we were racing, now onlookers gawk openly. This, however, is our biggest crowd yet – but as I send the lead skater of the Northanger Abbesses flying with a well-timed whack of my bustle, I only see one face.

Arthur is watching us – watching me – with a strange expression on his face. It's somewhere between fascination and longing and it manages what none of the Abbesses or Currer Belles have managed. It sends me reeling.

I stumble and find myself sliding along the ground on one knee, coming to a halt inches away from his (very nice) shins. I look up to see if he's laughing. Instead, he's smiling.

"Well," he says, "since you've gone to so much trouble to get down on one knee, I suppose I should say yes."

The world seems to come to a standstill for a moment.

"Well," I say, standing with a grace I wouldn't have thought possible a year ago. "That's settled then. Just make sure you don't arrange the wedding for a skating day."

After the Bluestockings race, shove and fight our way to a glorious overall victory, I resign myself to constant jokes about skating down the aisle.

In the end I walk, head held high, without my father's arm, but with a bright blue ribbon in my hair, a month after we fight our way to a bloody victory over the Currer Belles. I scandalise the guests by refusing to wear a corset, but my bruised ribs thank me for it, and at least the veil obscures my black eye.

"I was thinking," he murmurs after the vows have been said, the guests have left and we have indulged in a different sort of physical exertion altogether, "that I might get myself a pair of rolling skates and join you for a circuit of the park one day. How would you feel about that?"

I smile in the dark. "Only if you don't mind losing."

"If I did, would I really have married you?"

He's as good as his word, and when I wait on the finishing line for him to wobble up, breathless and laughing, I kiss him hard on the mouth. A Bluestocking is nothing less than gracious in victory, after all.

**Cariad Martin**

The door slammed open and a high-pitched groan of pain filled up our little caravan. The reverberation sent Mam's dream-catcher fridge magnets flying everywhere, and Dad spilt a cup of tea in his lap.

"Ma-a-am!" My sister, Skye, stood in the door way with her helmet and wrist-guards on, and a grimace on her face. "It happened again!"

Mam took one look at the blood pouring out of the gash on her arm and jumped up to run a clean cloth under the tap. While Mam waited for the water to get warm, Skye stumbled in on her roller skates. She collapsed down on the seat opposite me, sucking in air.

"Well, of course it's going to bleedin' hurt," Mam snapped, then cracked a huge smile. "You still can't make that corner then?"

Skye shook her head. "I keep taking it too fast and then forgetting that stupid manhole cover thing is on the racing line." She grinned widely at me, smiling through the pain as Mam picked out bits of grit from her wound.

Skye was thirteen, three years old than me and taller than most, with long black hair that she wore in two skinny plaits like Wednesday Addams. Mam finished cleaning up the cut and rinsed the bloody cloth in the sink.

"Are you both about ready to go?" she asked.

She didn't have her skates on yet but was wearing her derby clothes; a tartan skirt, red fishnets over black tights, and her training tee printed with the words *Gosker Rockers* over a rollergirl riding a Welsh dragon.

She didn't have a bout today, but she and Dad were coaching our Derby Brats team, The Gosker Lil' Rockers. I brushed off my red tutu and rolled out the front door, closely followed by Skye.

We lived in an old Airstream caravan on Nana's campsite in Tenby, which everyone at school thought was weird but it wasn't to us because it's all we'd ever known. Me and Skye shared the bedroom at the back, with twin beds and matching rainbow crochet blankets that Nana made when we were born. Mam and Dad slept in a fold-out bed in the gaucho, and then there was a tiny kitchen and a bathroom so small you could wash your feet in the shower and pee at the same time.

Skye was a jammer for our roller derby team. She's fast, and even with a grazed and bloody arm she easily sped away from me as we skated through the campsite on the way to practice. We rolled past Nana's farmhouse, and The Daffodil Restaurant & Bar where Dad worked six nights a week and came home smelling of vinegar and batter and salt.

An autumnal sun was setting in the clear sky and we blew up crispy orange leaves as we sped past. You could smell people's dinners creeping out of their caravans; all hearty soups and sweet roast veg and gravy.

Skye put her arm out to stop me in my tracks and made me listen to the sound of some bird I didn't care about. She wanted to be a conservationist when she was older and was always making me look at disgusting mud that was supposedly badger footprints, or deer poo.

I rolled my eyes and skated past her, putting the brakes on when we reached an old wooden board that read "Always Be Prepared." Mam's wheels stuttered to a stop behind us and she unlocked the doors to the old scout hut that Grampie and Nana had converted into a sports hall for campers.

It was mostly used for football, and for children's games on rainy days, but we used it once a week for roller derby, marking a track on the floor with orange cones and duct tape.

Dad was part-referee, part-coach, and after he laid out the track he crossed his tattooed arms and leaned back against the stacked plastic chairs, watching me and Skye do warm-up laps. Our black t-shirts were printed with our roller derby names; hers, Red Skye, and mine, Haf. Mam and Dad christened me Summer, but Nana started calling me Haf (Welsh for summer) as soon as I was born. In spite of Mam's protests, it stuck.

By the time our arms and cheeks were pink from the warm-up everyone else had arrived; a couple of girls from my class and a handful of Skye's friends, Helen Back, Rawrry Gilmore and Lucia Lightnin' Lopez.

They oohed and aahed over Skye's cut-up arm, and Skye acted like it was nothing. Teachers and classmates had been known to shrink in horror when she walked in to school with some beetroot-coloured scab on her face the size of a fifty pence piece, but Skye never made a big deal about it.

Dad blew his whistle and we all huddled around for instructions. Some of the girls were still new to roller derby, so we spent most of the first hour practising our blocks and safe, legal overtakes. For the last half hour Dad split the group in half, green bibs and pink bibs, and we had a mini bout. Skye was captain of the green team, and they won easily. She burned Roller Lola and Anne Explosion off the line every time it was her turn to wear the star-printed helmet cover.

At the end, Dad called us all round for a huddle again. We collapsed down on the gym mats Mam had put out so that the senior skaters could practise their jumps. No one had successfully landed one yet. I sunk back into the foam padding, laying my face against the cool, clammy blue plastic.

"Fantastic job today, girls," Dad said, and Mam stood beside him nodding. "You're all really coming along; I can't believe some of you couldn't even skate in a straight line without falling down only a few months ago."

A few pairs of eyes flicked towards Plucky Star, whose polka dot shorts had hit the polished wooden floor of the hall more than most during those first few weeks of practice.

"In fact, you girls are doing so well that we thought it was about time you had some other teams to play against."

Mam and Dad grinned at us, leaving an eager silence that we filled with hushed whispers. Skye twisted around to frown at me, skinny plaits flicking in the air, asking with her expression what they were on about. I shrugged.

"After hearing about our success, a couple of other local teams started up their own junior divisions. We've been in talks with them for weeks now and we've finally managed to get enough teams together to have our own Brats League."

The hushed whispers became squeals of excitement. Skye slapped her hand to her mouth. I jumped up and squeezed Mam around the waist, thanking her over and over.

"We didn't want to tell you until now because we didn't want to get your hopes up in case it didn't happen. But our first bout is this Saturday. We'll be playing here, against The Pembroke Rockets. Meet here at half-past eight for warm-ups, bout starts at nine."

Mam handed out letters for parents and we all got our coats and bags together, chattering excitedly about the weekend.

After practice we went to The Daffodil to get ice-cream milkshakes to celebrate; strawberry for Dad and Skye, chocolate for me and Mam. We sat at the bar and I rested my elbows on the coffee-coloured wood, blowing bubbles into my drink. I only stopped gushing about roller derby for about ten seconds, and only then because I was temporarily paralysed with brain freeze from drinking my milkshake too quickly.

"You were so fast today, Skye," I said as we got up to leave.

She smiled, pushing her bar stool under and licking the sweet, pink milkshake moustache that had formed above her lip.

"I mean, seriously fast. The other teams don't have a hope against us; we're going to win every match for sure."

I was positive of this, and couldn't stop myself talking about it. Even when Mam came in to tell us to go to sleep because it was an hour after bedtime, I was still bouncing up and down on my bed. I wasn't even a little bit tired, so I crawled in next to Skye, nuzzled against her flannel animal-print pyjamas and whispered until long after her yawns became deep, sleepy breaths.

Me and Skye travelled together in the mornings. Our schools were right next door to each other, so close they shared football and rugby pitches. Some of the girls from the team caught the same bus, so we steamed up the back window with excited chatter and laughter about Saturday's bout against The Rockets.

In maths class, I finished my test early but instead of handing it in and getting extra questions, I ripped a piece of paper out of my diary and drew a picture of what I was going to wear; black sparkly shorts with red and black striped tights. Skye had a pair the same so we could match. Hers had a ladder above the knee but it only made her look tougher.

Skye was sort of quiet on the bus home, but I filled the silence anyway talking tactics. She stared out of the rain-dashed window and nodded whenever I paused for breath, although that wasn't often. I told her about my plan for matching outfits, but she barely raised a smile.

"Are you alright?" I asked.

"Yeah, I am," she sighed, tightening her skinny plaits. "But I need to talk to you about some-"

She was interrupted as half a ham sandwich flew over our heads and stuck to the window with day-old mayonnaise. Half the bus cheered (the boys) and half the bus groaned (the girls) as the soggy bread and meat slid down the window. The bus reached our stop just as the mess slapped onto the floor, and we jumped down the steps to the glistening pavement, shouting '*diolch*' to the bus driver.

Skye popped open a polka-dot umbrella and we ran awkwardly home through the rain, bags digging into our sides and feet getting wet as we stumbled through shallow puddles.

We stopped running when we reached the cover of the bright red awning outside our front door. Grampie built us a deck outside our caravan before he died, and Mam had strung up solar-powered lights and pinwheels. In the summer it looked beautiful, with Mam and Dad sitting there in striped canvas deckchairs, watching me and Skye skate the concrete oval track around the campsite, practising our cornering and speed.

Skye shook off the umbrella as Mam opened the door and took our wet coats and shoes. On Wednesdays she only had to work until lunchtime, so three steaming mugs of hot chocolate were sitting on the dining room table waiting for us, and three cupcakes that she'd brought home from the shop where she worked. We changed out of our wet clothes and sat down at the table to tell Mam about our day, licking green butter icing and crunching sugar flowers.

"What about you, Skye, how was your day?" Mam said, licking icing off her finger.

"Okay," replied Skye.

She crumbled a sugar daisy to dust on the table, and Mam raised her eyebrows and looked to me for answers. I shrugged to say I had no idea.

"What's going on?" Mam asked, and Skye sighed and straightened up.

"They're going to start teaching advanced science classes on Saturday mornings at school, for the kids that are going to take their exams a year early." Skye tore the edges of the paper cake case as she spoke. "And you're upset because you didn't get into the advanced class?" Mam asked slowly. "Well, that's alright, love, you can take your exams with everyone else-"

"No, Mam, I *am* in the advanced class. I *am* going to take my exams earlier."

17

Mam's face broke into a smile that glowed, but Skye still looked miserable. I saw the problem, and spoke thickly through a mouthful of icing.

"But you can't take classes on a Saturday, we've got derby," I said.

Both Mam and Skye looked at me, then at each other. Mam put her hand over mine, and I felt the coarse sugar on her fingers.

"Haf, some things are more important than roller derby," she said, and I gasped and jumped up.

I looked to Skye, expecting to see her horrified, too, but she was looking down at her knees.

"Skye?" I said, backing away from the table. "You're going to tell them you can't take their stupid science classes, aren't you?"

Skye's chin scrunched up like paper and her lip trembled. Mam put her arm around my sister's hunched shoulders and hugged her tightly.

"You don't have to decide right this second," Mam said, kissing the top of Skye's head. "You can think about it. We'll talk about it with your Dad later, and we'll speak to your teachers and-"

"No!" I slammed my hand on the table and once again Mam's fridge magnets littered the floor as the caravan shook.

"Haf!" Mam shouted, her eyes full of anger like I'd never seen them. "That is enough. You go to your bedroom now and cool off, and we'll talk about this later."

"No. Skye, tell her. Tell her you're not giving up roller derby," I pointed at Skye, my hands trembling.

There was a lump in my throat like I'd swallowed one of the sugar flowers whole, and my eyes itched as I held back tears.

"Haf, please," Skye croaked, shaking her head. "You know I want to be a con- servationist, and my teacher said-"

"I don't care what your teacher said! You can't give up roller derby for some stupid... some FUCKING SCIENCE CLASS!"

It was the first time I'd ever swore in front of Mam, and as soon as I'd done it I knew I was in for it. Both Mam and Skye's eyes were wider than ever. Skye wasn't even crying anymore, but she looked terrified. Mam stood up and grabbed me roughly by the wrist. She didn't say a word, just dragged me to my bedroom and thrust me onto the rainbow crochet blanket. When I saw her eyes blazing as she slammed the bedroom door, I knew I'd be in there a while.

After an hour of lying on my bed silently screaming into my pillow, kicking the blankets and covers and generally working myself into a frenzy, I fell asleep, and only woke up when Dad came home.

He pushed open the door and I sat up with a start, the blanket stuck to my face with dribble. I wriggled against the wall, trying to make myself as small as possible for my telling off, but instead of getting cross he shut the door and lay down on his back on Skye's bed. After a minute's silence, I did the same, and we stared up at the low ceiling where Mam had strung up Nana's bunting and a set of yellow flower fairylights.

"Your sister is staying at Nana's tonight," he said.

I searched his voice for anger or disappointment, but he didn't seem either of those things. He even sounded a little sympathetic.

"She thinks you hate her," he continued, and turned his head to look at me for the first time. "You understand that she *is* going to take the Saturday science classes, don't you? She can't change that just because you're cross about it."

He put his hand out across the gap between the beds, expecting me to hold it, but at these words I rolled over and faced the wall.

"Haf…" he said, and now there was disappointment in his voice. "Her class starts at half-eight, so she'll be able to make it back in time to watch the end of the bout. She'll still be able to come for milkshake afterwards and celebrate your wins."

I closed my eyes and pretended to be asleep until Dad sighed, rolled off the bed and left me alone in the quiet darkness.

I left early for school the next morning and pretended not to notice Skye at the bus stop. She stood in a huddle with her friends and kept glancing over at me, but I laughed extra loud with my own friends and ignored her. The girls from the team were divided; most thought that Skye had sold us out and gave her horrible looks, but a few thought I was being a bully and stuck by her. The whole thing made my stomach ache.

Skye stayed at Nana's again on Thursday night. It was a chilly but dry evening, and I wanted to go out and skate for a while, but I was still grounded for swearing. Mam was so cross at first I thought she wasn't going to let me go to the bout at all. So I kept my mouth shut and settled down for a *cwtch* on the sofa with Dad, occasionally staring out the window at the crisp, starry night. Once or twice I thought I heard the gritty thunder of skates on concrete flying past our house, and bubbled with jealousy at the thought of Skye out there when she obviously didn't even care about roller derby. But then I told myself I was probably just hearing things, and fell asleep on Dad's lap to the closing credits of *Doctor Who*.

On Friday night, Mam let me go outside for an hour, to practise for Saturday's bout. The cold air felt weird on my warm, sweaty face. I tried to beat my record for the number of laps I could do without stopping. I did eleven, as fast as I possibly could, until my heart was thumping out of my chest and my throat felt dry. My eyes watered from the cold wind rushing into my face, and my legs started to go weak. Even though there were fizzy orange streetlights on each side of the road, I forgot about the manhole cover and flew over it at top speed. My purple plastic wheels screamed across the metal surface, I lost my balance immediately and smashed down on the floor. As I hit the ground, I couldn't stop a squeal of pain. My elbow was full of a strange sparkling feeling where I'd hit my funny bone, and I could already feel that my bum was going to be bruised from the square pattern of the manhole cover.

Hearing me yowling like a cat, Nana and Skye came running out of the back door of Nana's farmhouse. Nana yelled my name, dressing gown billowing as she skidded down the path in her slippers. I was still out of breath from skating so fast. Skye got to me first, and knelt down beside me to inspect the elbow that I was cradling.

"Get off," I hissed at her.

She pulled her hands away as if burned, and sat back on her heels as Nana fussed over me.

"I told your Dad this roller derby stuff was bloody dangerous..." Nana ranted to herself as she grabbed me around the middle and pulled my to my feet.

"Haf?" A small voice in the distance called my name, and we looked up to see Dad standing in the doorway of the Airstream, haloed by warm yellow light.

At the same time, I heard Skye sniff behind me, and I turned my head to see her running off back towards Nana's, braids flying behind her. Dad came to help Nana hold me steady, and as soon as I felt his big arms scoop me up I buried my face in his fish-and-chips smell and cried and cried until I ran out of tears.

Mam and Dad cleaned me up and put me to bed, hushing me when I insisted that it didn't even hurt that much and I'd definitely be okay to skate in the bout in the morning. I spoke between thick sobs and hiccups, and I thought they looked like they were trying not to laugh or cry as they kissed me goodnight and told me to just see how I felt in the morning.

When I got up I passed Mam's inspection of my cuts and grazes; my elbow was fine and the only thing that still hurt was the Tetris pattern of peanut butter bruises forming on my bum.

I padded into the kitchen in bare feet, holding the red-and-black striped tights in my fist. Skye was standing over the kitchen table putting books in her satchel. We both froze then carried on like we hadn't seen each other. I sat on the sofa and put my tights and trainers on, then tied the laces of my beloved, beaten purple skates together so they were easier to carry.

I caught Skye staring at the glitter-streaked laces, and the shabby purple plastic of my wheels. Dad strode into the kitchen and she snapped out of it.

"Are you ready, kid?" he said to her, and she nodded, slung her satchel on to her shoulder and followed him to the door.

After he walked out she turned back to me, opened her mouth, then closed it. She pulled the door shut behind her until there was only a millimetre of sunlight between the door and frame, and then flung it open again.

"Good luck," she said, loudly, looking me right in the eyes. "Tell everyone 'good luck'."

Then she left before I could say anything stupid or mean, even though I wasn't going to.


By the time Dad had dropped Skye off and arrived back at the scout hut, me and Mam had hung a huge, multi-coloured *'Derby Brats'* banner over the stage, and marked out the track extra carefully with neon pink tape that we'd bought especially for the occasion. We wrapped bright ribbon around the low beams and lined up a couple of rows of benches and plastic chairs for the parents.

When the team arrived there was a noticeable buzz in the air, an excitement so bright you could taste it. Everyone was wearing their best gear, and some of the older girls had sprayed colours and glitter in their hair. Lightnin' Lopez had even brought fancy new skates, and had worn them non-stop for three days to wear them in.

The excited hum was silenced only for a moment when The Pembroke Rockets arrived. I knew from going to Mam's bouts that the rivalry was only pretend (most of the time), and that quite often the players on the other team turned out to be your best friends. But even so, I couldn't help narrowing my eyes as they piled in to the hall, shyly following their coach and the few parents that were helping out.

Their kit was blue, a bubblegum ice-pop blue, and almost all the girls wore the same star-patterned knee-high socks.

Mam, Dad and The Rockets' coach called us all around for a huddle said they wanted a good clean bout and told us to do our best and have fun. I took the opportunity to eye up the competition.

Both teams were split into two: juniors (under 13) and seniors (13-17). I had to stop myself groaning when The Rockets' I Scream Sundae put on the blue star-print helmet cover and lined up on the start line for our junior jam. She was at least as tall as Skye, and looked about twice as strong.

The jams weren't as speedy and wild as Mam's bouts. Actually, a lot of the time the pack looked like eight newborn deer wobbling their way nervously around the track. The Rockets won the first jam easily as I Scream Sundae powered her way past our players. Our Lightin' Lopez was actually quicker once she got space, but she struggled to fight her way through the slow-moving, shaky pack.

Luckily our over-13 team was more evenly matched. Without Skye, our best jammer was Polly Pocalypse, and she was about the same size, shape and speed as her rival point-scorer.

The two age groups took alternate jams, and both teams won a handful each. After a brief blackcurrant squash and custard cream break, we were back on the track. I lined up in the pack next to The Rockets' Misty Moon, a blocker with giant hair like red fusilli pasta and the most freckles I'd ever seen on her nose. She had complimented my skates while we were lined up in the toilet queue, and I said I liked her bracelet that looked like Dolly Mixtures. She smiled at me until the whistle blew, then her eyes went serious.

I saw the giant, looming shadow of I Scream Sundae behind me, and tried to blow myself up like a balloon to stop her coming through. I weaved left and right, feeling a rush of air as Lightnin' Lopez flew between two of The Rockets' blockers and did a breezy lap of the hall, sticking close to the inside of the neon pink tape track.

"Yes, Lucia! Come on, Haf!" A familiar voice yelled from the small crowd of parents on the benches, and I looked up long enough to allow I Scream Sundae a way through. She sped off and I tripped and skidded on my knees, still searching the crowd for the source of the cheering.

I looked up and found Skye's grinning face, standing on a bench and waving like a fool. Nana was sat next to her, tugging her school jumper and telling her to sit down. Skye gave me a double thumbs-up and then allowed herself to be dragged down by Nana.

White-and-blue skates appeared in front of me and Misty Moon extended her freckled hand to help me up. I brushed off my legs and realised I'd laddered the knee of my stripy tights. Now Skye's pair and mine really did match. Misty Moon skated away, and I caught up with the pack for the last fifty seconds and stopped I Scream Sundae scoring any more points.

While the seniors took their places on the track I rolled over to Skye, nearly knocking her over with the impact of my rib-cracking hug. She smelled like school.

"How was your class thing?" I asked, trying hard not to sound sarcastic.

"Bo-oring," she said, rolling her eyes. "I'd much rather have been here."

We turned our heads as the crowd noise got louder; both jammers had broken through the pack and were speeding round for another go.

"But I have to do it," Skye carried on, raising her voice over the cheers and keeping one eye on the jam.

We stood with our arms around each other's shoulders while both teams scored twice each and tied up the scores, before Dad blew his referee's whistle.

"Do you think I'd make a good jammer?" I said, rolling backwards towards the track to take my place for the last jam of the bout.

Skye paused for thought. "Yeah, I think so," she said, nodding confidently. "I was watching you last night out of Nana's bedroom window. Before you slipped on the manhole you were skating super-fast. Maybe even as fast as me."

I grinned, tuning in to the faint, throbbing pain from the peanut butter bruises. Helen Back shouted my name and told me to hurry up, so I glided back to the starting line. We all leaned forward a little, anticipating the whistle.

"Ready?" Dad said, from the other side of the pink tape.

I looked over as he put his whistle to his mouth, and smiled back when he winked. As the room went silent I bent low for a quick start, and heard a crackle as the ladder in my tights stretched even further up my leg.

**Robyn Frame**

*Zero-Sum (adjective); of, relating to, or being a situation (as a game or relationship) in which a gain for one side entails a corresponding loss for the other side. "There must be one winner and one loser, for every gain there is a loss."*

Everybody has had one of those practices. The ones where you'd rather sit for an hour and a half with your finger shoved in your eye than go through that again. And they're always the practices that have everyone else glowing and mewing with joy. The second coach blows her whistle to signal the end of practice, I disappear to the other end of the sports hall. The others are all ecstatic. The hollow feeling in my chest is something I'm familiar with; the disappointment of two hours pushing yourself and gaining nothing. But two years into my derby life, I'd expected these experiences to become fewer and further between.

I try to untie my skates. But the faster I try, the more complicated the knots become and I'm on the verge of chewing through them when Dstryr flops down next to me and wipes her sweaty brow.

"Wow," she says, unfastening her helmet. "Great practice."

I can't even look at her, that's how much I want to punch her. Dstryr never has a bad practice. She's that girl, the one who is better than you and she knows it. She knows you know it, too, and she will rub it in your face at any opportunity. I look up to and admire all of my teammates, with the exception of Dstryr, who I wouldn't piss on if she was on fire. "You smell like the inside of a kneepad," I tell her, and go back to untying my skates.

She narrows her eyes, jaw clenched. "If you want some tips on J-blocking ,then I'm happy to help you out," she replies, packing her skates and pads Tetris-style into her bag. "It's pretty tricky to stay on your feet the first time you do it."

"It's not the first time I've done it."

"Oh. Right." She puts her mouthguard back into its case which she in turn tucks into her bag. She doesn't look up and meet my eyes, but I can see her smirk. She knows how long I've been tackling J-blocks.

"Do you have a massive bottle of Patronising Bitch before you come to practice every night, or what?" I snap, yanking off my skate with the laces still tied. I feel betrayed by my equipment. I'm so busy fuming I don't see Astrid glide over. She sits down between Dstryr and me, a gentle hand on my arm, just above my elbow pad. She's barely touching me but a shiver runs the entire length of my body. I shove everything into my bag and zip it up in silence.

Dstryr looks like she wants to say something else but Astrid's expression warns her not to. She leaves without saying goodbye and Astrid heaves a sigh. "I wish you wouldn't talk to her like that," she says, in her 'I'm-not-angry-just-disappointed' voice.

"She's a douche, Astrid."

"She's my friend, Sarah."

Whenever I was naughty as a kid, my mum would call me by my full name to drive home the scale of her anger. Nowadays, I know I'm in trouble with Astrid when she doesn't use my skate name. I swallow and nod, get to my feet and shoulder my bag. "This again."

Astrid doesn't look up, doesn't rise to the argument I'm spoiling for. "Just ignore her. It's easy enough. It's like you seek her out just to pull this kind of crap. It's not her fault you had a bad practice."

My hands curl into tight fists for one, two, three seconds, then relax. "I didn't have a bad practice."

"Oh, please," she rolls her eyes, standing up and brushing off her shorts. "It was written all over your face. You need to learn to smile through the pain," she says, sweeping her hand in a circle around a wide, toothy grin.

"Your mum needs to learn to smile through the pain," I mutter, holding open the door for her as we head towards the car.

The next day, at work, I'm bordering on homicidal. Last night's practice plays out in my head like a rubbish made-for-telly film. By now, people's heads should turn when I walk into the hall because I'm the one to beat. But instead they're casting glances because they're waiting for me to come up against Dstryr again, waiting to see what new illegal procedures I've invented just so I can attack her.

I *try* to see the good in her. I know Astrid wants me to. But I can't see past Dstryr's douche-baggery. A lot of the time, it's not even me that instigates the arguments, or the deliberate shoulder-checks to the jaw. That gets on my nerves. But Dstryr was there before me. Long before me. And Astrid will always side with Dstryr even if she pushed me down a flight of stairs.

When you're dating a rollergirl you have to accept from the outset that your relationship will always be more of a threesome than anything else. She'll always love you but, if derby came first, you might always come second. She might spend more time with you than her teammates but what she shares with them will seem to matter more. In those couple of hours, blood, sweat and actual tears are shed. It's like *Fight Club* on eight wheels – who you are when you're on the track isn't somebody your lover knows.

Unless they're a rollergirl too.

I met Astrid in a pub a couple of weeks before the team had their Fresh Meat intake. I've never been one of those girls who chats up strangers at bars, but I remember thinking that if I didn't approach her, I'd regret it for the rest of my life. Trying to act cool, I'd gestured at the throng of people on the dancefloor and asked her.

"What do you do when you're not doing this?"

She smiled disarmingly and leaned in. "I'm a rollergirl. I play roller derby."

I was drunk and brave. "Do you want to come home with me tonight, rollergirl?"

She smiled, tucking a stray curl behind her ear. I abandoned my friends and let her lead me out of the pub.

After that we hung out whenever she wasn't at practice. When she was, I'd drive her there and sit on the balcony overlooking the sports hall and watch. I was happy doing that until she bought me rollerboots for my birthday. "It's your turn now," she said.

Fresh Meat sucked. I spent most of my time staggering around like Bambi trying desperately to stay upright. I persevered though, and I understood that it wasn't meant to be easy. Whilst I was learning T-stops and four-point falls Astrid would sit whispering with her teammate who was taking notes on our progress, looking up at me every now and again. The pressure of her gaze made me stumble.

After that first session, Astrid introduced me to her teammate who looked me up and down with an unreadable expression. Astrid smiled warmly, "This is Dstryr," she said and the other skater stuck out her wristguard-covered hand to shake mine.

I mashed my hand against hers, intimidated by her height and demeanour, and mumbled my name.

"I'm Astrid's derby wife," she said. I had no idea what that meant but it sounded too much like infidelity for me not to frown, giving Astrid an accusatory glance.

"I'm Astrid's real-life girlfriend," I told her, aware of the edge in my voice.

Dstryr laughed, "Yeah. I know. I guess that makes you the bit on the side, right?" It might have been meant as a joke but I couldn't have laughed even if it had been funny. I knew right away we weren't going to get along.

At my minimum skills assessment, I knew the endurance laps would be where I'd struggle most. Dstryr's comments didn't exactly fill me with confidence. She sucked her teeth and shook her head, saying it was hard work. As if I didn't know that already. I was convinced she'd fail me even if I managed seventy laps in five minutes. I said as much to Astrid later, in the car on the way home. She laughed, her knees drawn up to her chest in the passenger seat, messing around with my radio.

"Nobody would do that," she said. "Nobody is that spiteful."

I disagreed. Suddenly the hot topic at fresh meat was no longer the girl who could do thirty laps in five minutes, it was me. Other newbies didn't want to be my partner because I had a reputation of being a bitch, and our coach would glaze over when I was talking. Loose lips sink ships, and Dstryr's well-aimed remarks about finding my attitude too negative were certainly sending me down to the depths. I dread to think what she said to my teammates when I wasn't there, but I doubt it was very flattering. And that negative perception spread like wildfire.

All around me the bridges were burning and I was powerless to stop them, because every time I saw Dstryr's face I wanted to punch her. She would make snide comments about my fitness, about how little I had progressed. And whenever I opened my mouth to retaliate, Astrid would appear, her hand on her arms, fingers pinching a warning.

I didn't realise, then, what I was coming between. Contrary to popular belief, my dislike for Dstryr had been immediate and sharp, not some long-stewing hatred born from jealousy of hers and Astrid's friendship. I know Astrid's life didn't start the day we met. I knew she had friends and past relationships, scars and medals. Accepting that derby was always going to be a huge part of her life hadn't been hard because before long it became a huge part of mine. But accepting Dstryr gave me a new-found sympathy for people who murder their families.

The following night, I park outside Astrid's flat and trudge up her path. When she answers, she glances over my shoulder at my car parked a foot away from the curb, then back at me.

"You park like a joy-rider."

"At least I can drive."

She smirks humourlessly and locks the door after her. At the car, she dumps her skate bag beside mine in the back before sliding into the passenger seat. She sniffs the air, then glares at me.

"I thought you said you quit smoking."

Shit. It was my new year's resolution, something I knew would only make me a better skater, but after a week of biting my fingernails down to bloodied stubs after arguments with Dstryr I gave up giving up. "I say a lot of things."

"Will you promise me something?"

"Depends."

"You have a choice. You can either stay away from Dstryr all night or you can be civil with her."

"I'm always civil with her," I lie. Astrid sighs heavily. I turn my head to look at her, then back at the road.

"Despite what you think, I don't play derby on the off chance I might knock her teeth out. I go because I love it. Derby, I mean, not knocking her teeth out. I go because I want to become a better skater., But then she comes over and says stuff like 'yeah, J-blocking is always hard first time round' when she knows I've done it a million times before. It's... what's the word...?"

"Disparaging?"

"Yeah. That. And she'll be having a go at me and then you'll come over and tell me off. She loves it."

"I don't tell you off," she protests, weakly.

I almost choke trying not to laugh. "You do."

We sit in silence for the rest of the drive; she doesn't even adjust the radio tuned into Smooth FM – Barry Manilow playing just audible enough to be annoying. Music as wallpaper, Astrid's called it before, and I know it grates on her. But tonight she crosses her arms petulantly over her chest as we carve our way through the darkened streets to the leisure centre.

It's not until we're sitting in the car park that she speaks again. I kill the engine and roll up the window I'd opened to get rid of the smell of stale cigarette smoke. When I go to open the car door her patient hand is on my arm, fingers falling into place over the bruises. "Don't you think we should quit?" she says. "You know, while we're ahead."

"Quit the league? No way." I turn and hold both her hands in mine. "We're both doing really well. You're amazing. A-team amazing. And I have it all to play for now with the new teams being picked next month. And you'll easily be voted captain, no doubt about it."

"I don't mean the league," she says, pulling one hand away to push her hair behind her ear. It falls in her eyes again, and she pushes it back.

I stare at her blankly, trying to read her expression in the dark car with only the sickly yellow glow of streetlights around us. "Astrid?"

"I mean us," she looks up at me, her eyes glassy with tears. "I think..." she pauses, choosing her words carefully. "I think we should break up."

I feel like someone has sternum-checked me into a wall. It's that same sinking feeling you get when you know you've committed a penalty, before the ref blows the whistle.

"Sarah?" she says, gently. "What do you think?"

I pull away from her, physically reeling from the hurt, and get out of the car wordlessly. She follows me and I lock it, dropping the keys twice as I try to put them in my bag. I walk up to the entrance robotically. Astrid is a foot behind, calling my name. I turn around, but I can't meet her eyes. The anger is so strong I might be sick. But when I open my mouth, all that comes out is a meek little voice, one that isn't my own, saying "we're going to be late." I spin around and walk inside, plastering my face with the fakest smile of my life.

I make it all the way to scrimmage without incident. Still, smiling is making my face ache and I can't look directly at Astrid. We end up on the same team, so

I make sure I'm in a different rotation to her. That way we won't have to skate together. My head hurts; a dull pounding behind my eyes. I take a long swig of water and pinch the bridge of my nose.

"You okay?" asks Sue Narmy.

"Yeah, fine," I say, and she looks at me with disbelief. "I'm good," I say again, firmer this time, and snatch the pivot panty from her hands before skating toward the track and joining my team. They're on the back line, lowered to one knee.

"Five seconds," one of the referees calls authoritatively, raising his hand. Then the pack whistle blows.

I can feel my heartbeat in my throat. Our jammer shoves her way out of the scrum of blockers and disappears down the straight. When I catch sight of the opposing jammer, Kat Astrophe, in my peripheral vision, I swoop in for a J-block but misjudge it, hitting her in the face with my helmet instead.

The referees would've sent me off if she hadn't gone down in an arc of blood, her hands coming up to cup her mouth. Around her, everybody takes a knee. She pulls out her mouthguard, gleaming and stringy with saliva and blood, and mumbles "M'okay." I want to apologise, but if I speak I might cry, so instead I focus on the blood climbing the cracks between her teeth and shining on her lips. Eventually she gets up and returns to her bench, the skaters there enveloping her in a circle of kind questions and gentle pats on the back.

I'm still on one knee when Dstryr appears, her crotch directly in line with my eyes. She looks down at me with her hands on her hips. "You have to go to the penalty box," she says incredulously, practically frothing at the mouth with rage. "Just because the ref hasn't called it yet doesn't mean it wasn't a penalty."

"Yeah," I say quietly as I get to my feet. My head is splitting now; it feels like someone is drilling behind my eyes.

She has her back to me and isn't talking to anybody in particular when she says, "Should be expelled anyway, that was definitely on purpose."

"Pardon?"

Dstryr glances at me over her shoulder. "You did that on purpose," she says, slower this time. Swivelling round to face me, she smiles, but it's all mouthguard. It makes her look like a bulldog sucking a lemon.

I'm about to tell her where to go, but instead I shake my head and skate to the penalty box. I run the cord of the stopwatch between my fingers and watch the seconds tick by. It dawns on me that if this jam is called off before my time in the sin bin is up, I'll have to skate with Astrid. I'd rather drink a bottle of bleach. In fact, that's pretty tempting, even more so when the penalty whistle blows and Dstryr gets sent off for a back-block.

Picking up the other stopwatch, she spares me a sideways glance that I don't have any desire to return. "I think Kat Astrophe's face has stopped bleeding," she says. I don't even look at her. With her free hand she pries her mouthguard away from her teeth and wipes it absently on her T-shirt. "Do you know what the score is?"

"Black are on who-gives-a-toss and white are on why-would-I-care." I flash my big, fake smile and go back to my stopwatch. This is the longest minute of my entire life.

"Don't get ratty with everyone else just because you got dumped," Dstryr snaps, putting her mouthguard back in and sucking on it noisily.

The dislike that started the second she spoke to me like I was five years old now boils over and I calmly put my stopwatch down and turn to her. I want to put into words how belittled she makes me feel, how she came between me and Astrid from the get-go, how hard it is to drag myself to practice knowing she'll be here, but I can't. I open and close my mouth like a dying fish and she smirks. She actually smirks. And that's what sets me off.

I'm not a violent person. Before roller derby I'd never so much as shoved anyone, as much as I'd have liked to. Now, though, I find myself slamming my open palm into her face. It's more than a slap; it is the metal splint of my wrist guard smashing into her nose. She shrieks in pain and falls away and I get up as calmly as I can manage. There's a moment of silence as everyone stops and looks over at us; me standing over Dstryr as she curls up on the floor, crooning in pain and clutching her face.

Sue Narmy hurries over, demanding to know what happened.

I just shrug and pull off the pivot panty, making a beeline for my bag. Astrid goes to follow me, but then she sees the blood on my hand, on my wristguard, and stops. She frowns, like she's about to say something, but I cut her off.

"I quit," I tell her. "While I'm ahead."

This time the laces of my skates come undone easily and I take off my pads under the watchful eye of almost the entire league. I should feel ashamed, especially when I see the look of utter horror on Astrid's face. But it's just a bit of blood, and that's what we all signed up for. They're acting like I've walked in on Christmas Day and pissed on their kids.

I get up and shoulder my bag, checking I've not left anything because there's no way I'll ever be back. I don't even look back on my way out. I know it won't do me any good. By the morning Chinese whispers will have changed this from my unruly temper flaring up to a full-scale assault, and I find it hard not to smirk at the idea. Let them talk.

I don't skate for a while after that, retiring my boots to the cupboard to gather dust. The good thing about living in a city is that one league is only a stone's throw from another, but the downside is that everybody knows everything. I doubt my misdemeanour with Dstryr will have gone down any better than a lead balloon.

I pluck up the courage, eventually, and turn up with my skates and kit in one hand and my heart in the other at a leisure centre similar to the one I used to practise at. The captain of the team looks me up and down. "We don't want any trouble here, she says sternly. No-one's going to want to skate with you if you're a douche."

I nod dumbly, unable to speak. Somebody has filled my mouth with cotton wool. Behind her the skaters are kitting up for practice, men alongside women. She follows my gaze over her shoulder and smiles. "We're busy nurturing a merby league here too. We're growing. Rollergirls are a dime a dozen these days, so you have to prove yourself to us."

I'm scared by how much I want this, need this, crave this. I give her a smile, a genuine one. I want her to know how much this means to me, her giving me a chance. "I won't let you down," I tell her.

She laughs. "Get your kit on before seven or you'll be doing fifty press-ups," she says, walking away.

I don't make the team and it makes me feel suicidal. It's my own fault, I suppose, for what I did to Dstryr. Even if I could do twenty-five laps in five minutes with my skates on my hands, I wouldn't have made the team yet. Everyone's still waiting for an Incredible Hulk explosion of rage. I'm happy now, though, away from Astrid and the others. I just don't know how to make them see it.

It gives me something to work for, though. And it's exciting. The other skaters are kind, if not a little wary, but they still invite me out with them after a bout and I accept. Most of the skaters are already in the pub by the time I'm finished helping tidy up the sports hall after the game. People think roller derby is sexy but most, if not all, of the girls declined the possibility of a shower in favour of getting here faster to cram in more drinking time. Their make-up is smeared, their hair flat and messy from their helmets.

After-parties are always messy and I never was one to say no to a bender, though skating with a hangover is the kind of punishment reserved only for the deepest circles of hell. I order another gin and lemonade anyway, watching the merby boys throw some serious shapes on the dancefloor. They look more like they're trying to keep steady in an earthquake.

Across the dancefloor, a girl catches my eye and looks away, then back. I smile, trying to look inviting. But I'm still not ready when she approaches and says hi.

"Hey," I reply, trying to act cool. In the process my elbow slips from where I was leaning on the bar and I spill most of my drink all over the floor. I wince. "I won't be offended if you want to walk away now."

She laughs. "I'm Lauren."

"Sarah."

"So, Sarah, is this a work night out?" She asks, glancing around at the derby girls chasing each other around the pool table with the little blocks of chalk.

"Nah. They're my teammates," I tell her. "I play roller derby."

Her expression changes from one of mild interest to one of intensity. Exactly the way mine did when the same words spilt from Astrid's mouth the first time that we met. I try not to feel smug, but it's hard.

"You're a rollergirl?" she asks. "That's... that's really cool."

I know. "Yeah. It really is."

"Do you want to come home with me tonight, Sarah the Rollergirl?"

It takes a moment for these words to register in my head. But when they do, I smile, telling myself not to look desperate. I set down my three-quarters-empty glass and tell her that I'd love to. I let her lead me from the bar without looking back. I'm already praying she never puts on her own pair of skates.

**Kylie Grant**

I wake early. I've been waiting for today for what feels like forever. In reality, it's only been four months. Four months of longing for one crucial game. Four months of counting down the days, crossing off each one. The Frimley Fractures are going to crush the Windsor Whips. We're going to win; there's no doubt about it. Sherry isn't going to know what hit her.

It is late summer, the dawn just beginning to shed light on the suburban roofs, making the world feel alive. I open the window. The air is cool and I imagine for a moment that I can see my breath before it disappears. When Sherry stayed over last winter, we always woke early and would open the window and pretend to smoke. Breathing vapour out into the darkness, her mouth, wet with sleep and dreams, drove me crazy. I was eighteen and desperately in love. She was twenty and restless. We talked about nothing but roller derby.

This morning, I'm alone. Sherry hasn't slept over since the spring. I can no longer hear the faint snores and movements coming from Sherry as she slept on the spare mattress that lay across from mine. She has defected. Her betrayal so complete that it was almost unbelievable. Sherry was always one for surprises. But now it's my turn. If it all goes to plan, the winning streak of her new team – all tousled, pure-bred long hair, pretty manners and toned thighs – will come to an end. I want to cause her pain. And the only way Sherry will hurt is if she loses.

Sherry is the best jammer I know. She is wiry, fearless, risky. Her derby name is Wild Whippet. I remember I laughed when she told me. The name reflected her so perfectly that I just couldn't keep a straight face. When she skates, she knows the audience can't take their eyes off her, as she writhes and winds herself through even the tightest block. She is pure entertainment, pure strategy, and pure calculation.

I loved her the moment I saw her out on the track, it was my first training session and she had me hooked on derby in an instant. Her power was so completely out of sync with her thin, taut body. It always caught the opposition off guard, no matter how much they had heard about her.

I'm known as Squint Eastwood, on account of my need for contact lenses and my obsession with Dirty Harry. I needed a new name after a bust-up with a rival team who wouldn't allow Blind Fury due to it already being taken by one of their blockers. Sherry came up with Squint Eastwood one day as we walked home from training; she whispered it in my ear. The name stuck, and so did her voice.

I move away from the window and close my eyes against the impending daylight. I picture Sherry cracking her knuckles through clasped hands, the hollow snap of bone against bone as she readies to take off. I see her sly smile as she drops her eyes to the track before lurching forward into the noise.


That day, I could barely concentrate on my classes. They dissolved down to white noise; an indistinct rumble in my ears, ears that were already full of chants, cheers, and the vibrations of skates on a track. And Sherry. Her voice like rain on a tin roof, forcing itself into my consciousness, and making all other sounds meaningless.

On my lunch hour, I call our coach. Just so I can hear skates in the background and someone other than Sherry. She asks if I'm okay; she knows me well and can sense that I'm tense, but I fob her off and mention that I've got exams coming up. She knows about Sherry and me of course, everyone does. The team tried to shield me from the worst of it at first, tried to tell me Sherry had quit rather than leaving us for our arch rivals.

Only one girl blamed me for breaking the unwritten rule, the rule that stated that you should never fall in love on the track

The coach tried to sit me out of this game, saying I was too close to it, that I would do almost anything to win. But to tell the truth, I think it's the reason I'm still in. It will be my first game as a jammer. No one else could replace Sherry. There's no one else quite so close, or with quite so much at stake.

As I walk to the game, I can feel my muscles tense and my pace slow. I run through positions and tactics in my head once more, my body responding by arching and tightening as I walk. The day Sherry left me she kissed me so hard my lip bled. She didn't need to say anything.

The roar of the crowd penetrates the changing room. As a local team we have a loyal following of loud women. All shouting, all clamouring to be heard, and all ready to fight. Frustrated women always make the best audiences.

The tension is building inside the room; the coach has already been in to run through strategy for tonight, the spaces on the track where we all need to be. Her eyes lingered on me.

We help each other to get our gear on. They don't mention Sherry. Our pivot Terri watches me closely. I can feel her wanting to comfort me but also wanting to keep me distant, for my anger to maintain its natural rhythm. I smile and she returns with a broad one of her own. Terri is a PA in her other life, a PA to some dumb fuck she says, although she won't say who he is. She never tires when she skates, unlike some of the others; her momentum always steady and strong, her legs taut, her arms at perfect angles. But sometimes her eyes glaze over. It's then that I like to think she is imagining skating over her boss, wheels leaving marks on his skin, carving his body into pieces.

We skate out onto the track, the crowd roars and I see my first glimpse of Sherry. She's laughing with one of her teammates. Laughing like nothing has happened. Like the last four months are just time passed. I feel the hairs on the back of my neck bristle.

The referee blows the whistle and we all get into place. Wild Whippet lines up next to me. Her body is stronger than when I last saw her; her legs heavier and her shorts tighter. She reaches out to shake my hand. One of her fingernails lightly scratches my palm when she retracts.

The first whistle is blown and the teams begin to move off. The Frimley Fractures all in violet. The Windsor Whips in yellow, their scrubbed skin pale against their shorts. A double whistle blows and I can't see anything else but Wild Whippet's skates in front of mine. My head fills with the noise from the crowd and I push forward. My legs burn, my stomach lurches and I reach the pack just before Wild Whippet. One of the blockers from Windsor Whips moves quickly and stops me from swinging around one of her teammates. An arm hits my helmet and I feel as if I'm falling.

Terri moves behind me and straightens me up. I watch as Wild Whippet is pushed into the middle of the pack, unable to get around. I'm shunted through to the edge of the pack where I can speed up. Some bitch in a yellow tutu holds herself in front of me. One of my blockers attacks her and a space opens. Wild Whippet comes from behind, forcing me to slow my pace. She sprints and then she's lead jammer.

My brain screams that it's not over, and my body immediately responds; my legs push harder and my arms tighten. Wild Whippet is slower than usual, and I quickly overtake. I watch as her smile hardens. She won't let this go without a fight. We sprint back to the pack, and she's careful not to push herself too hard. She isn't as risky as I was hoping she would be. I can see the sweat as it runs down her legs, creating a dark patch at the top of her pale yellow socks.

We get to the pack together and I lose her. A tiny girl in a yellow leotard pushes me, her small hand coming down hard on my hip. I turn to force her off, but she's clever and already her hands are nowhere near me. Velociraptor, a blocker on my team, and Terri have trapped Wild Whippet in a tight formation, and they're both increasing the pace to control her.

It's now or never and I make my move.

I put my head down low and push as hard as I can. I overtake two of the Windsors and one calls me a cunt, the word lingering in the air a moment before I tell her to fuck off. All I can see are wheels and track. Someone pushes me forward and I know I'm nearly free of the pack, but something else is happening. I can hear screams. The referee blows the whistle. I put all of my weight on one foot to slow myself and then turn. There on the floor is Wild Whippet.

Blood sits on the track. Wild Whippet is covered in it. Her pale skin bloodied. The referee is too busy to notice as I reach down and pick up what looks like a white pearl, one of Wild Whippet's gleaming teeth. The room fills with noise; boos from the crowd, and recriminations from both teams. A first aider helps Wild Whippet to her feet and off to the side. I turn away.

Wild Whippet is replaced by some posh bitch with hockey legs who I know I can beat. She isn't a scratch on Wild Whippet. I know I can beat anyone now, especially with Sherry's tooth in my pocket and her blood on my skates. Velociraptor smiles at me, and I notice how her smile is slightly crooked, and wonder if she has plans for the winter.

The whistle blows.

**Steven LaFond**

Monster's kneeling in the corner lacing up her rollerskates. Her arms shame most of the men at my gym. Tattoos of goblins and witches dance across her biceps, and a single scar darts out from her hairline to her left eyebrow, from the time she slid off the track and into the stadium stair railing. Before each bout, she rubs lipstick into the scar so it can be seen from the stands. There are metal washers, old wheel bearings and chicken bones tied into her dreadlocks.

Monster plays in the People's Republik Derby Dolls, the flat-track roller derby league of Cambridge, Massachusetts. In this league, each roller derby team has a theme. Monster's is called the Zomb Squad, their shtick being that they're un-dead pin-up queens. She's also Jaime Tillman-Pointier, my wife. When she's not crashing into other women on rollerskates, she teaches digital photography to high school students. Her students and co-workers often come to watch her play. Derby has given her a reputation for being tough, and it's given her cred with the athletes and roughnecks who'd normally give her trouble in class.

I arrived an hour early to the auditorium to reserve the best seats. The stands are general admission. There's a VIP section, but it's not worth the cost to sit right next to the crash zone when I can get a seat with a better view of the whole arena. Just before the bout starts, I run down to the floor and rap my knuckles on her helmet. With so many people around, it's not like I could hug her. Don't want to make her seem less scary. "You going to kick ass out there?" I ask.

She tosses her helmet at me and stands up. Her face looks different when

39

she wears her red contacts. More angular. *Beastly.* In her skates, she's as tall as I am, six-foot-one. Her green and black uniform is tight; bringing home that her body is more muscle than bulk. With her build, Monster'd have no trouble defending herself in a fight. And that's the way I like her.

"I'm nervous tonight," she says into my ear. "Have you seen my dad yet?"

I shake my head. Her parents have never been here before, but after nearly two years of inviting, begging, and pleading, Peter bought a ticket for tonight's bout. We were both surprised. Her mother claimed she had a deadline and couldn't make it. Diane Tillman is the author of the feminist bible, *The End of Eden.* The friends of mine that went to college are impressed when they hear she's my mother-in-law. I'm relieved she's not here.

"I'm saving a seat," I say. "I'll let you know when he comes in."

The crowd around us is already amped. It's going to be a good night. By the way she begins looking over my shoulder at the scoreboard, I can tell she has to get going.

"Okay," I say. "I'll be up there yelling for you. Make their mommas cry."

"Every day," she says.

Tonight, the Zomb Squad faces off against the Razor City Renegades from Manchester, New Hampshire. With ten minutes until showtime, fans are filing into the stands. My seat is only one row behind the home team's bench. I reserve the spot to my left with my bomber jacket, making sure Peter will have a good view when he gets here. I almost cover the space to my right for Papa out of habit. After a year, I still catch myself doing it. It's not like I have to; the seats next to me are rarely in high demand. I know what some of the people see when they look at me. Big bald guy, angry, boots. *Skinhead.* Fuck these people. I know who I am.

Every tenth member of the audience holds signs for the Zomb Squad. I'm a big dude but Peter's even taller than me, about six-foot-seven, so I should be able to spot him. I'm wearing my Zomb Squad t-shirt with "Mr. Monster" in big white letters on the back. It suits me fine.

After a quick introduction of the visiting team, the Zomb Squad skates through the curtain, the spotlights illuminating their first lap of the track. The fans wail when the announcer screams, "Number 13, *MONNNNNNNN-STERRR!*" She skates ahead of the pack, fist in the air. I'm looking past her, toward the door. Peter's still not here.

Monster takes her position on the starting line, thick thighs tense underneath green fishnets. At the first whistle, she smashes into a player from the opposing team. The girl rolls to the floor, skates in the air. Monster smiles as she comes around the corner, black mouthguard making her look toothless, inhuman. The crowd stomps and screams. Some guy sitting behind me taps me on the shoulder.

"You must be that girl's biggest fan," he says.

"She's my wife."

The guy does one of those long whistles and says, "Right on." Then he starts asking me how the game is played. He's new to the sport and doesn't understand how teams win or lose. Wherever the fuck Peter is, I have no idea. A huge hit on the track gets me to my feet.

"Fucking hustle, Zomb Squad!" I yell. Then I try explaining to him that each team has five skaters on the track. The Renegades' jammer almost gets through the pack first. Monster's teammates surround and slow her down, allowing Shortnin' Dead, our jammer, to speed through the pack unopposed. "That's who scores the points," I say to this guy, taking a moment to cheer before explaining that she'll get a point for every member of the opposite team she passes.

"How can I tell?" he asks.

"The girls with stars on their helmets score points," I say. "No star means blocker."

A referee sends Witch Hazel, one of Monster's teammates, to the penalty box for elbowing one of the Renegades in the stomach. The call's bullshit. I start yelling at the outside referee, Remington Neil. "Get off the track, asshole!"

A Renegade player rams into the back of one of our girls, sending her crashing into the VIP section seats. There's a loud "ooooh" from the stands. Thankfully, Neil sees this and sends the Renegade to the box.

"Finally! Do it right, dick!" I scream.

"I thought they could hit each other," the guy yells in my ear. His breath smells like dog shit. "They could when it was on TV."

"There are legal hits," I say. "But that ain't one of them."

"Then how do you know which is which?" he asks.

I pick up the programme I got for Peter and hand it to him. "This will explain it better than I can." He still doesn't shut up.

"Can they pull hair?"

The Renegades' jammer cuts the track and is given a major penalty. I get up and cheer and the prick and his buddies at least clap before he taps me on the shoulder again. Yes, a jammer can be sent to the penalty box. No, there are rarely fistfights. *Of course it's real.* Then he starts talking about how most of the girls are pretty hot.

"Your wife's pretty fast for such a big girl."

"The fuck you say to me?" I ask.

"Well, come on, dude. She's a really big woman." He says. His friends try to keep from laughing.

"Most of the girls are really hot, but –" he says.

Muscle memory is a funny thing. I'm up and turned around before I remember I'm in public. He's a chubby little guy, maybe five-six, wearing a Bruins t-shirt and white jeans. White jeans. His ratty mullet looks like a wig. I want to rip it off his head. It only takes a second before he knows he's stepped in it. He keeps his eyes on my chest while stammering an apology.

"Find a new seat," I say.

"Dude," he says. "No offence or anything. Let me buy you a drink."

"Get out of here," I say. "Now."

He gets up and his friends stand up with him. My shoulders are almost wider than the two of them. The one to his left eyeballs me for a second. His mouth's tight, like he's holding back a threat he couldn't possibly carry out.

"Something to say?" I ask. None of them reply.

They leave, and with them gone, I look at the people behind. They're staring at me with that uncertain look of disgust I've always hated. Let them judge. I avoid looking anyone in the face as I sit, not because I'm afraid of anyone, but because I know I won't let it stop at a stare down. Monster looks up into the stands and notices her dad's seat is empty. For a moment she loses her game face.

It takes a few minutes for me to calm down even a little bit before I check the score. We're ahead. That relaxes me a little. Had Papa still been alive, he'd have been right there next to me, giving that prick hell with me, maybe even throwing the first punch. Monster's parents are college professors. They don't appreciate how I take care of business. Papa was a barber. He knew what was up. You don't suffer fools.

Growing up, it was just my grandfather and I in Putney, Vermont. Most of our neighbours were hippies. Papa was a veteran of the Korean War, and a lover of Frank Sinatra. We hunted every year of my life – even when I moved out of state. Jaime loved him; in spite of him being the kind of man her parents feared. To them, he was the enemy, the old generation who voted Republican and owned more guns than shoes. In truth, the man was raised a New Deal Democrat. Papa called us the "real Vermont". Not the transplants and ageing baby boomers, but the descendants of fur trappers and Huguenots. But I will say one thing for my in-laws: at our wedding, Jaime's mom hugged Papa as Peter welcomed him to their family. It was a gesture, if empty, that kept the surface tension of the day in place.

The first year Jaime started playing roller derby, Papa drove down for every game to watch his granddaughter-in-law skate. Six hours round trip. The ladies in the league loved him. He had watched roller derby a few times on TV in the 1950s, and would tell them of the time he saw a live bout with his army buddies. When he died alone in the house he raised me in, Monster and I were headed to an away game in Philly. We didn't find out until the next day.

No matter how fast the Renegades are, Monster and the Zomb Squad catch them up. She gets in front of them and then slows down, bending over, getting her ass in their way. Everyone in the sport can "booty block," but when Monster does it, she seems to take up half the track. At the end of the jam, one of the Renegades Monster's taken out throws her helmet to the floor and starts swearing at the referees, landing her a gross misconduct. Monster looks up at me before she takes her seat on the bench. She's covered in sweat and panting. I call her father's cell and he doesn't answer. I call his house and Diane picks up.

"Is Peter on his way?" I ask.

"That was the plan," she says, "but he has to do some errands first."

"Errands?"

"Did you call him?" she asks.

"I did. But wanted to make sure he didn't leave his phone at home. Did he?"

"Keep trying him," she says. "I have to go. "

Jaime had hoped that tonight would be the bridge between her dad and me. This could've been the moment where Peter and I could sit down, as men, and just enjoy the night. I wonder if Papa would appreciate how I'm handling this. If there was a problem, he and I would just hash it out. But Jaime's parents aren't like that. They're *civilised* people. You can't yell at them and then have a drink to make it all okay. There's no way I could give Peter a clip on the ear to straighten him out. If I snap, it will only prove to him I'm not a rational human being. And I can't let him or Diane get that satisfaction. Jaime has taken so much shit from her parents from the moment she first brought me home four winters ago.

I had arrived at their big green house that evening, dressed in my best bowling shirt and jeans. I hadn't known what to expect. Jaime and I had met on the internet, on a forum for hardcore punk fans. We loved the same bands, movies and books. I looked at their property. Papa's house could've fit inside their driveway. Peter greeted me at the door and gave me a close-lipped smile while shaking my hand.

"May I take your coat?" he asked.

He brought me into the kitchen where I met Diane. Diane took my hand with a firm grip and said she had heard a lot about me. I told her about the friends who'd loved her book.

"Did you read it?" she asked.

The urge to lie was pretty powerful, but I couldn't say I had. She nodded at that and asked what I did for a living.

"Computer consultant."

"Wow. That takes a lot of schooling," Diane said.

"Maybe for some people," I said. "But I learned the real way, by actually doing it."

That last bit hung in the air for far too long. As we ate dinner, I tried talking about football.

"I haven't watched it since high school," Diane said. "Too much going on in the world."

"Teaching college," I said, trying to change the subject. "I can't imagine how you can teach all the students you do. How do you keep them interested?"

"Well, you learn how to reach them by actually doing it," she said, then took a sip of wine. I couldn't tell if she was joking with me or just being insulting.

Peter stifled a smile and handed me a roll. Peering at my right forearm, he read my tattoo aloud. "Body Count?"

"It's a band," I said.

"You love them that much?" He kept staring at the name.

"I did at eighteen."

Diane laughed. She asked, "You couldn't have just bought a shirt?"

"They hate me," I said to Monster later.

"You're sweet and funny and smart. They'll warm up. You're –"

"Backwoods?" I offered. "White trash?"

"Not what they expect."

She told me stories about how when she was a kid, she would pretend to be Spiderman and ambush her father in the hallway of their house. They would play-fight for hours. Her mother had sewn her tutus, a Batgirl costume, and several other outfits she'd play and sleep in. I loved these strangers she talked about. Where were they every time we would go over for dinner, when I'd sit there and eat as the conversation drifted to thoughts about art, the theatre and politics? Several times, Jaime attempted to get me involved in conversations, but I was either ignored when I had a different opinion, or would offer only one-word answers. Eventually, Jaime would go to her folks' house alone. She'd tell me they asked about me, but I had my doubts they really cared. "How is he doing?" most likely code for *"when will be out of our lives?"*

A year into our relationship, we let them know we wanted to be married. The stillness of their kitchen, which was where all family business was conducted, was the first indication this was not happy news. Peter grumbled weak congratulations and gave me a limp handshake. Her mother reminded Jaime to keep her last names, both of them.

After our honeymoon, I noticed a shift in Jaime whenever she spoke with her parents. Before we were married, she'd get off the phone and happily relay whatever news they told her. Now, she would hang up from phone conversations sad and dejected. Work had gotten worse, too. She no longer mentioned students unless they were the bad ones. She gained weight and talked about it constantly. I didn't know how to fix it, so I did nothing.

One night, Jaime woke me up out of a dead sleep to ask me if she was boring.

"All I do is grade kids' artwork, tell them to sit down and keep busy before the bell rings."

"You're a teacher. That's your job."

"I think my clothes are dull."

"It's two in the fucking morning."

She rolled over and said nothing else.

After that night, we stopped fucking. She began eating two or three cupcakes a day, which only caused her to get sadder and fatter. Time away from our apartment became a relief.

Desperate, I went to my in-laws and told them about my worries. Peter asked if I had done anything to make her upset.

"We fought for months after I shrunk her favourite t-shirt," he said.

"I don't do the laundry," I said.

"What do you think is the problem?" Diane asked.

"She's sad." I said. "This shit between me and you isn't helping."

"And what exactly is happening between you and me?" she asked.

"Come on," I said. "Meet me halfway, Diane. I'm searching for a way to fix this crap."

"Then take a breath," Diane said. "We are talking about Jaime, here. Calm down."

"Well fuck, this isn't going anywhere," I said. I got up and made my way out. It was another moment of feeling stupid for even trying to talk to them. They had raised her to believe that art and higher education would light a path to a successful future. Perhaps she'd have found someone else with a creative job, or decent teeth, but instead she married me.

One night I came home from the gym to find her watching a TV programme about roller derby. When I asked her what she was watching, she shushed me and I found myself getting sucked into the show too. Badass women, knocking the hell out each other, yet still friends in the end. Cool. During one of the commercial breaks, she turned to me and said "I could do that."

The game's getting tighter than I would like. The Renegades rally in the middle of the period and are able pull off these really smart plays, scoring three or four points a jam and then calling them off before we can widen our lead. Our team's not talking to each other. A *"Let's go, Zomb Squad"* chant starts up, and I join in and forget Peter as best I can. Two minutes later, and we're only ahead by seven points.

When the half-time buzzer sounds, I make my way through the crowd and slip through the blue curtains used to section off part of the auditorium from the public. I knock on the dressing room door and it's answered by Matilda Grrrilla, a blonde skater with a monkey tattoo. "Monster," she calls over her shoulder. "Your man's at the door."

I tell Monster I spoke to her mother and that her dad is on his way. She kisses me and tells me I need to fuck off while they discuss their strategy for the next period. Rather than go back the way I came, I take the utility hallway out of the auditorium and wait for Peter outside by the front doors. This way I can spot him more easily and hopefully get him seated before the next period starts; before he causes more harm than just breaking his daughter's heart.

Within a week, Jaime found the derby league in Cambridge. She decided to try out. I encouraged her. To prepare, she trained six days a week, both on skates and at the gym. When tryouts were held, she made the cut and started dragging me along to help out. I volunteered for every job the league needed doing, from bout production to security. On days when there were no practices, she skated in our apartment building's parking lot and I let her bang into me as hard as she could. One morning, I noticed that the refrigerator shelf Jaime had used to store cupcakes was filled with V8 cans. It was unexpected and awesome.

"You're kidding me," her mother said when Jaime brought them a flyer for her first bout. Jaime assured her it wasn't a joke.

"No, it's wonderful," Jaime said. "It's all skater-run and owned! There's the travel team, which goes all over the nation, playing against other teams. It's going international."

Jaime really sold the female empowerment angle. Watching Diane scratch under her eye thoughtfully, I hoped she'd break down and be happy for Jaime. Maybe I'd get a glimpse of that woman who sewed costumes for her little girl at last.

Her father snatched up the flyer, looked at the skaters on the front and clucked his tongue. It was apparent their uniforms weren't acceptable to him.

He asked, "Since when did fishnets count as sports equipment?"

"Don't worry about that," Jaime said. "Some people just like wearing them."

"And the crowd loves it, I'm sure," Diane said.

The two of them weren't listening. Jaime's enthusiasm was rapidly going away and she was getting really quiet.

"Fuck it," I said, standing up. "Are you two finished shitting on this? Because I'm pretty tired and we'd like to go home."

"Is this how you leave every conversation here? 'Fuck this and fuck that?'" Diane asked. "Sit down."

"No, we're done," Jaime said.

Diane pointed to my empty chair. She said, "Let's talk this out."

"We have to go," Jaime said.

"Sit down," Diane said. "We don't leave conflicts unresolved here."

Grunting, I turned my neck to the side and heard it crack. Nobody appeared to like the sound. Peter stood up and put his hand on my shoulder and told me to relax. I pushed his arm away, maybe too hard. He almost fell over, his face all screwed up in surprise. I had fucked up.

"Whoa," I said. "Sorry."

"Get out before I call the police," Diane said.

I apologised to Peter again, and he whispered the "it's okay" you get from someone when it isn't. Jaime stood up and left with me. She didn't talk to me much that night. After a few weeks of no contact, we resumed visiting her parents' home every other week for dinner and pretended that night had never happened. I could tell by the way they watched me that they saw me as a danger, to them, their relationship with Jaime, and perhaps Jaime herself. I was the pit-bull that had finally snapped its jaws.


Now, after about two years of me going to their home and going out of my way to show them that I'm not some violent redneck, they're attempting to make peace with Jaime's decisions and with me. I'm proud I keep myself in check and hope they realise I'm not some ogre. But none of that shit's going to matter if Peter doesn't get to the auditorium.

The sun's going down. I check my phone's clock every thirty seconds. Peter's prompt when he has to be somewhere, so this is insulting. The auditorium doors open and I see that dick from the stands and his two friends come out. They're staring at me and I'm trying to ignore them while I look at the time. I'm overhearing bits of conversation. The words "asshole," "Nazi," and "faggot" come up more than once. It'd be so easy to sort them out.

Half-time is almost over before my phone starts ringing. Peter sounds upset. He's got to get home, he tells me. He's remembered they need groceries for a dinner party tomorrow night.

"No," I say. "You're coming here."

*"Excuse me?"*

"You said you were coming. Now my wife, your daughter, is looking up from her game into the stands every ten minutes look at your empty fucking seat, and we might lose."

"I'm the only person who can go to the store right now."

I breathe in deeply and swallow every curse word I can.

"Tell me what you need," I say. "I'll get it."

"I'll try to get it done and get there before it ends," Peter says.

Looking over my shoulder I notice the dicks are still out here and I can't be sure if they're waiting for me or not.

"I need you to be here, Pete," I say. "Please."

Within ten minutes, he's in front of the auditorium and I'm escorting him inside. The teams have taken their place on their benches.

"Your seat is over there." I point at the stands behind where Monster's standing. He nods and hands me his grocery list. It's not in his handwriting. Without thinking, I hug him. He tenses up in my grip, but I get a slap on the back before I let go.

"You're – you're doing the right thing." I say. "I can do this and get back here before it's over."

It's a five-minute drive to the nearest grocery store, and ten minutes of shopping. I spend most of it trying to find the brand of couscous Diane printed on her little list. Another fifteen minutes and I'm in my in-laws' driveway. Diane runs out onto the porch.

"What are you doing here?"

I pop my trunk. "Helping you while your husband plays the supportive father."

"He *went* there?"

"Help me with this shit, please."

When we get in all the groceries, I check the time on my phone and realise I'm not going to make it back before the end of the bout.

"Would you explain to me how he went shopping and you came back?"

"I convinced him that his little girl was looking forward to seeing her dad in the stands. He agreed it was important."

"Listen," I say. "Imagine the look on her face if you came back with me."

"Are you really asking me to go with you?" Diane asks.

"It would mean everything to her," I say.

When I get back to the auditorium people are starting to trickle into the parking lot. I run in, knocking a few shoulders. The MVPs are being announced over the PA. I look at the scoreboard and smile, the Zomb Squad rallied and handed the Renegades a big defeat, 151 to 86.

Monster's in the centre of the track, posing for photographs with her fans. Some lesbian with a flattop throws one arm around her for a picture while a little girl (the lady's daughter, maybe) stands in front of them both. Monster pretends to bite the kid and gives her a hug. Without the fans, Monster's told me before, she's just another big girl; too wide to be a model, too weird to want a normal life. But here, she's adored. Men and women, chant her derby name and hold up signs saying, "Make Mine Monster." Although she's married, she gets asked out more than she ever did before, which I think is another reason I love this.

Peter stands a few feet from his daughter. He's taking in the way people treat her and can't hide the pride on his face.

"How did you like it?" she asks her father.

"It was-" he says, with a pause. "It's not what I thought it would be. It's exciting to watch. But it's still frightening to have you knocking around people and getting knocked around yourself." He looks at her forehead and frowns. "You got hurt again?"

"No, it's make-up," she says.

Peter licks his fingers and tries to wipe the lipstick off her brow. Monster slaps his hand away. She turns bright red and asks him to stop, but she's giggling when she does it. Peter looks at me for a moment and rolls his eyes. It's not all that hateful a gesture when he's in a good mood.

"Your mother should have seen this," he says.

"Next time," she says.

"Jaime the derby girl," he says.

"Monster," I say.

We make our way to the auditorium's function room where Peter starts asking us questions about the game. I answer them as best I can. Something inside me feels different, like a dam broke in my chest and it's emptying into my guts. Peter's constant eye contact through our conversation is unnerving. The smile on his face is more so. His phone's vibrating in his pants pocket. Peter doesn't go for it. Trouble will be waiting when he gets home.

Just outside the doors, the dick in white jeans and his friends are waiting in the lobby. They're trying to get me to notice them. We lock eyes as I feel Peter's hand slap my back. My neck goes stiff, like a dog straining at the leash. I hope it holds.

**Evangeline Jennings**

This is what I do.

I muss Amy's hair and promise I'll see her the far side of the weekend. She tells me to break a leg, but not my own. Even after nine months on the heart-breaker ward, these are the moments that rip your soul apart. This beautiful twelve-year-old girl will never go home again, yet all she cares about is my welfare.

God knows it isn't fair. But my parents taught me long ago – fair died.

I see my reflection in the dull steel of the elevator doors and I'm not impressed. When they open, Amy's family steps out. Perfect.

They're perfect in every way – other than Amy – but they don't hold it against her. They've come to eat a home-cooked dinner with her. After dessert, her little sister will ask for help with her homework. And later, if Amy's still awake, they'll watch a movie together. Something wholesome and lovely with a very happy ending. Something to keep the nightmare at bay.

"Hi, you. How's she doing?" Polly is Amy's mother. It's obvious where the kid gets her good looks. And her charm. I don't care what the redheads say, blonde is beautiful. Anything else will never be any better than second place.

"She's had a very good day." I can smile because it's true. "You'll find her in decent spirits." I hope. "But be careful, please, not to overtire her. You know how fragile she is."

Of course they know. She's their daughter, and they're very good parents who spend as much time with her as they can afford. But still I have to say it. Because it's what I do.

Polly smiles to show she understands all the above – and why I have to say it anyway. For a moment, I think she might hug me, but she doesn't. Her husband's mind is elsewhere. There's a pretty student nurse at the drinking fountain. Word on the ward suggests her breasts are real.

As I strip off my scrubs, I shake off my respectable veneer. Shuck my professional image along with my Crocs. Motörhead plays something loud deep inside my skull. I arch and stretch in the mirror and begin my metamorphosis.

It starts with the simplest thing. I swap my white underwear for black.

When I get home, I find a letter by the side of my bed. Baby never opens them, but she always leaves them somewhere for me to find. I take it into the kitchen, put the kettle on, then tear the old man's letter to shreds and feed it into the garbage disposal.

"Baby?" I shout. "You home?"

"In here." The bathroom, of course. Where else would she be?

"You want a mug of coffee?"

"Please."

When I take her coffee in, she's neck deep in the tub. Blonde hair billows across the surface of the water and her left nipple winks at me as the bubbles ebb and flow.

"You going to be long? We have to leave in an hour. And don't forget, I still need a shower."

"Not much longer, promise. Get out my clothes for me?"

"Sure." Why not? I bought her a new pair of fishnets on Wednesday night.

Thick socks. Sheer footless pantyhose. Fishnets. Skirt. T-shirt. Tank top. Turtle shell bra and panties. Her gear is laid out on her bed when she pads into our room. We still have twenty minutes. Not too bad for her.

She drops her towel and pulls on the panties I picked out for her.

The line of her leg. The curve of her ass. The flat of her belly.

Baby is as beautiful as ever.

Fair died.

Bitch ran off all the hot water.

Scrubbed and shivering, I dress in a hurry. My fishnets are ripped and torn. I pull on leggings instead. Strictly speaking, Baby and I are wearing the same uniform but if you saw us together you wouldn't think we even belonged to the same species.

She looks like sex on skates. I'm death on legs.

Our apartment is close by the hospital in the heart of New Troy. The bout is at a warehouse on the far side of the river. The drive to Bakerline is forty minutes. My truck, my rules, my playlist.

Bikini Kill plays *Rebel Girl* and I get into character.

Baby brushes her hair and stares out of the window.

I'd skate through a brick wall for her.

The only thing on Baby's mind is winning.

Winning and finishing prettier than the rest.

Courtney Love is screaming when we pull into the lot. Am I pretty on the inside? I don't think so. Fuck it, let's be honest, I'm not even sassy.

A bunch of teenage fan boys spot Baby as she slides out of the truck. They want autographs, photographs, and a slice of celebrity skin. I let her sign their arms, and shirts, and papers. I don't let them any nearer than necessary.

Baby loves their attention. It tastes like victory. No longer a jobless runaway from a rundown mining town, she's Baby Amphetamine, Metropolis Roller Derby's lethal Lolita. She's a star, and she adds her shirt number to every autograph she signs. She wanted to wear 130 and have me take 75, but I had something different in mind. She's 300-62-9.

One kid in a Pearl Jam t-shirt asks me who I am.

The next guy in line warns him off. "Dude, that's Girl Eleven."

Pearl Jam takes a step back. "Everybody hates you," he says.


Both teams skate warm-up laps before the doors are opened. The hospital is important in my life and the apartment is my refuge. But this banked track is the only place I ever feel truly alive, and I stay out when the rest of the girls go back to the locker rooms. In many ways this is the best part of my night.

Our bout tonight pits MRD's champion team, Bad Mothers, against the heaviest hitters in the Gotham league, the Guttersluts. It's an invitation exhibition contest.

Cruising in off the curve, I notice one of the Sluts leaning on the rail at the side of the track. She's built like a big brick shithouse and I guess she's heard about me. If looks could kill I'd be sixty-six feet under.

The doors are open now. Punters are streaming towards the bar. A dozen – maybe more – have stopped to watch the freak skate.

On the PA, Ani Difranco sings *Amazing Grace,* but in my mind Lemmy is shredding *Metropolis* and I'm allowing myself to get medium angry. Who the fuck does this bitch think she is?

I angle my approach so it takes me right alongside her.

She's still staring me down. Not a quitter.

I smile – all friendly like – I'm sure we can be friends – and as I roll past I coldcock her, clean on the side of her jaw with the meat of my elbow. I spin away from the impact and head for the locker room. The Gutterslut goes down in a heap.

I hope the cameras caught that. It'll look really cool on the next Bad Mothers YouTube compilation.


The captain of the Sluts comes into our locker room to complain about me. I'm listening to the Beastie Boys on my headphones but I learned to lip read at an early age. Girl I hit goes by Mountain Olive. She's pissed and spitting feathers. Feathers and blood. Things are about to get medieval.

BJ Harvey, my captain, looks over at me with outstretched arms and shows me empty palms. *Dude! What the fuck?*

I shrug my shoulders back at her. *Bitch had it coming.*

Then BJ asks the Gutterslut: "What makes you think *I* can control *her?*"

The Beastie Boys tell me *She's Crafty*. I was only doing my job. The job BJ asked me to do.

The Slut turns on her heel and leaves angry. The name on the back of her shirt reads Lezzie Boredom.

Apparently, it's on.

Another week in the life.


My Bad Mothers shirt sports the classic Ace of Spades. The slogan underneath is Born To Lose – Skate To Live. The bout starts in forty-five minutes and I'm in my quiet place when Baby slips out of the locker room through the fire escape.

Do I follow her?

Yeah. Of course I do.

She's gone when I get outside but I find her in the old accounts office. Perched on the edge of a table with her skirt around her waist and BJ's head buried between her thighs. She looks at me and smiles. One hand on her breast. The other in BJ's hair.

I wipe away the tear before it has time to escape.

Baby's eyes roll up and her orgasm rages.


Roller derby is a magnet for freaks of all sizes and shapes. Although I'm sure it's not polite to call them freaks. What I mean is, here everybody's welcome. Nobody's judged. And the violence is restricted to the track. It's somewhere even Venus can feel safe. It's steaming hot in the Metrodome tonight – the walls are sweating – but she's still wearing her floor-length rabbit fur coat. Ditto her Cossack hat and matching muff – no sniggering at the back. I know she's naked under there – we've all seen her penis – but it all seems a little extreme on a night like this. I guess maybe that's the lady's point.

"Ladies and gentlemen," our MC announces. "Your penalty referee tonight is none other than the lovely, the gorgeous, the divine Miss Venus In Furs. Guttersluts, beware, if you haven't been told already, Miss Venus is really very strict indeed. And please don't be fooled. Miss Venus may speak softly, but she carries a surprisingly big stick."

It's funny because it's true. Venus is hung.

The crowd is still laughing when he introduces the teams. I wanted our theme to be *Ride of the Valkyries* but, as so often happens, I was outvoted. Instead, we're telling our fans to get their freak on.

Baby leads the way. It's a given. The sway of her hips. The thrust of her chest. Her do-me-hurt-me clothes. There's a blatant sexuality about her – a vibe derby fans have always picked up on. Tell them she was coming hard and long against her captain's face thirty minutes ago, and they wouldn't be surprised.

They might be jealous though. Baby brings out the possessive side in almost everyone. Of course, the ones that don't love her typically want to hurt her. That's where I come in. The punters watch her skate. I watch them.

Two gay boys we know from the Rainbow Cattle Company Bar and Grill offer Baby a large bouquet of flowers. It's a prearranged stunt and a cheap photo-op for Metropolis Roller Derby. This sort of thing plays well with the bloggers and alt-press. It's hard to capture the speed or violence in a single frame, but give them a pretty girl in a tiny plaid skirt and their editors will run with it every time. There's even talk of a TV documentary.

One of the boys is wearing the full-on Amphetamine outfit. His legs are good, but Baby's are better.

As Baby approaches the Gutterslut fans that have made the trip to the Apricot, a couple of drunks are up on their hind legs and shouting. The first word I hear is 'skank'. Another might be 'die'. I move up the line a little, but trust her to deal. Baby stopped being helpless the first time she said no.

She plucks a couple of roses out of her bouquet, skates over to her hecklers, and presents them each with one. Everybody cheers her and she curtseys before she blows them all a kiss.

Compare and contrast.

"You! You fat bitch! Olive is going to fuck you up. Just you wait and see." A lanky streak of piss from Gotham leads my ritual abuse. I won't win him over with roses, and it's still against the law to kick his ass. So I stop and stare at him. Count slowly up to ten. Then hock up a good one and let it fly.

The crowd goes wild again, but definitely not in a good way.

Venus shows me a yellow card. And her penis.

When the Guttersluts skate in, they're accompanied by an industrial metal version of Wagner's finest. Colour me unimpressed. Democracy is severely over-rated.

The big chick I decked skates at the front of the Guttersluts pack, waving a sledgehammer high above her head.

"Olive! Olive! Olive!" Her fans chant and pump their fists in the air.

They have fun, fun, fun until Venus takes the hammer away.


Baby and I sit out the opening jam. It's something we like to do. See what the other team has brought and talk about our tactics while we armour up with all our protective gear. Olive is solid, but angry. Too angry to be smart. She trips Fat Tuesday and tries to stamp on her. The Sluts rack up a one point lead, but Venus isn't stupid. She knows this is going to get nasty and puts Olive in the stocks to set an example.

While the crowd howls its approval, she throws a couple of cabbages and an overripe tomato, before showing Olive the obligatory penis. Strictly Metropolis rules.

The stocks are in the centre of the track. I consider taking Olive out while she can't defend herself. But it's a coward's trick and it's time for the next jam. Olive has to watch from the stocks.

Baby has the gold star on her helmet. BJ is our pivot. My job is very simple. Do whatever needs doing, and do it hard.

Lezzie Boredom is jamming against Baby. She must be ten years older but she still looks pretty hot. Long legs. Tight butt. And an angry intense scowl. None of that helps her at all. Because Baby leaves Lezzie in her wake as they race towards the pack. Fuck, that girl can skate. She makes me proud.

As she sweeps towards us, BJ and I open the inside channel. A move we pull at least once every bout. We fake to the top of the boards and then plunge down. Every manoeuvre is clean and completely skate legal. First we zig inside the four Gutterslut blockers and then we zag out again, taking two of them up to the rail using only their own momentum and our shoulders.

My mark bounces back off the barrier, loses her footing, trips, and face surfs along the boards. I hurdle her and skate on – there's no need to break her head, it's only the second jam. BJ's girl goes over and lands in the second row.

Baby flies past on the inside. She's so far ahead by now, we don't try to slow

Lezzie down. The crowd has seen their violence. Now let them watch two hot chicks skate as fast they can.

Bad Mothers score an easy four points. Baby puts her hands on her hips to call off the jam before Lezzie can even make it back to the pack.


Third jam, Baby is rested. I'm not. BJ wants my protection. The DJ plays Alanis Morissette.

Coming round the top curve with thirty seconds left, I see Olive fronting Baby on the opposite side of the track. The final pieces slide into place and I hip-check a Slut to send her sprawling out of my way. Face plant.

I'm a machete cutting through pig fat as I slice through the pack and come down off the bend like a runaway rollercoaster. When I hit Olive they feel the impact back at stately Wayne Manor. I tackle her round the hips and take her down hard. We narrowly miss a cameraman as we tumble. Olive's head bounces off the concrete – that's why we wear helmets – and I have her by the throat before she regains her senses.

"Don't. You. Go. Near any of our jammers ever again. Next time I see you bother either of my girls, I'm going to fucking kill you. Understand? Rip your fucking head off and shit down the hole."

Every skater and referee in the house comes to Olive's rescue. The crowd laps up the ensuing brawl. Venus banishes me to the Flying Cage.

Before she turns the key, I get a thanks-but-what-the-fuck hug from Baby Amphetamine.

The only thing I tell her is: "Pull out of the next jam."

When it starts, I'm in the cage. Suspended twenty feet above the track. This is where I'll be the next two jams. One more foul play tonight and I'm banned from our next bout. That's OK. I think my work here is done.

Standing on the line, Olive looks up at me and slices her throat open with a finger. Girl got game.

When the pack starts to roll, Olive doesn't move. Then she spits her mouth guard out and turns to charge the Bad Mother jammer.

BJ has nowhere to go.

Olive hits her hard and rag dolls her. Butts her in the face and rains punches into her ribs until finally her own team pulls her away.

The medics carry the casualty towards the management office. Olive is banished to the locker room.

Game over.

Bad Mothers win the bout by twenty-eight to five.

I haven't been to a party since I left Kentucky and locker room celebrations are always too loud for me. These days I prefer quiet reflection. And anyway it's time to reverse my metamorphosis and ease back into my other self – the normal – the everyday me. I can't be Girl Eleven anywhere but here.

BJ is at the ER with her husband JT, but the rest of the team is high on victory. Baby is at the centre of it all. How can we be so different? I leave her to the limelight and step through the fire escape for a much-needed post-bout cigarette.

Olive comes round the corner, pauses, and then joins me. She's out of character now. Ramones shirt, jeans, and battered biker boots. Her hair is surprisingly long. She scrubs up very nicely.

"I needed some fresh air," she explains. "Got a light?"

"Sure."

"Got a cigarette?"

We both laugh. I offer her the pack. She takes one and I hold a match for her. She cups her hands around mine to protect the flame from the wind. Draws the smoke deep and exhales through her nose.

"Well played," she tells me with a rueful smile.

"Thanks." I say it carefully.

"No. Really. Very well played. I mean it. You whipped my ass out there. Totally Sun Tzu."

The best thing I can say to that is nothing.

"Looking forward to the rematch?" She isn't threatening me, it's conversation.

"Wouldn't miss it for the world."

"Me either. Should be real."

"Yeah. It should."

"When is it, do you remember?"

"Four weeks from today."

"Cool. Well, don't go breaking a leg or anything important before then."

"I don't plan to." Not my own, if that's what she means.

"Good." Her grin is almost malice-free. "Because I'm going to be gunning for you in the worst possible way."

"I wouldn't have it otherwise."

"And." She hesitates.

"Yeah?"

"Lezzie and me. We waitress some nights at a place called the Chili Hut. It's a hole in the wall with some pavement by Salmagundi Square. That's where we like to wind down after a bout. You and Baby want to, be welcome to come along."

"Thanks. That'd be cool. We could make a weekend of it. No one breaks a leg or anything important, it's a date."

We smoke our second cigarettes in silence. It's a knack. When the blast of a horn breaks the comfortable peace between us, Olive grins. "That's my cue to go."

She grinds the last of her cigarette beneath the heel of one of those big boots and we hug it out for a moment before she leaves. Her body is warm and fleshy and rock hard underneath. That rematch is going to be a challenge. She pecks me awkwardly on the cheek, and then punches my arm.

"Been a pleasure, Girl. Be seeing you."


As I pull the truck out of the lot and point it towards the bridge, Baby asks the question I've been expecting. "You set BJ up, didn't you?"

I shrug. She knows the answer. All warfare is based on deception.

She stretches for my knee and gives a gentle squeeze. "You're so silly. But I love you. And I promise I'll never leave."

Baby doesn't get it. She never has. I don't care if she leaves. I only want her happy. That's all I've ever wanted, from the start. To protect her, keep her safe until she finds her happy ending. Baby deserves more out of life than I could ever provide. But giving herself to every using bitch or bastard that wants inside her is not the way to repair the damage the old man did.

I turn the music on. Courtney sings about clouds. I think it's a metaphor. Probably.

When I stop to pay the toll on the bridge, Baby is already asleep. She's innocent and lovely as a child is meant to be. Better late than never, I suppose.

I wonder about taking her in to see Amy. I've already promised to show the kid all the bout footage when the company gets it up onto YouTube early next week. Amy might be excited to meet the star of the show. Especially if Baby wears her uniform.

I'll run the idea past Baby before I ask Amy's parents. I'm confident her father will approve.

*Good Sister/Bad Sister* is the next song up.

**Magda Knight**

"You want milk? Go on, girl; tell me you want milk."

As I hunch over my bar stool, the bartender's question catches me off-guard; I can only assume I look like someone in dire need of milk. The seemingly-innocent question is laden with veiled threat, much like everything else in this shitpuke enclave. Ensconced between the rope-bridge estates of Ill-Stockwell and the sub-terranean battle-labyrinths of Brixton-Gone-By, Pinktown is a far cry from the cosy matriarchies of Malden New Eden or the Urfields in London's East End. There's no yarnbombing and "grow the wheat and turn the other cheek" here. There's no love thy neighbour, even if they draw a gun on you, because *aww*, they've had such a *hard* life, and surely one taste of your wholegrain sorrel croissants or perfumed welcome crew will show them the error of their ways.

No. Pinktown is a deathzone, plain and simple, geared towards prestige and power. A hard place betrayed by the marshmallow softness of its name.

I like milk. It's refreshingly lacking in discrimination, available in a spectrum of fats, not genders. I may have entered this hellzone to perform one last little wet-job, the assassination of the jammer of the Pinktown Hellcats, but that doesn't mean I can't enjoy cool white slipping down my throat, a creamy moustache on my upper lip.

My body *yearns* for fats and vitamins I've long since forgotten the name of.

"How much for a shot?" Despite myself I lean forward for the answer.

"Haw! Fooled ya. Milk's off."

The bartender sports lank hair of indeterminate colour weighed down by grease and a trucker cap. Weathered skin, heavy slab of a face. Hunting knife on a waist belt, the blade used for purposes other than vanity, judging by the unshaved moustache and aged pubic-tough whiskers round the chin. A walkie-talkie clipped to the forearm for easy access and regular communications. A demi-boss, then, ordered to vet road rats like myself for signs of trouble.

No-one can say I don't aim to please. If she's looking for trouble then I'm highly inclined to make some. What if I hold a knife to the bartender's throat? Is she the boss-dog? Will she sling me out? Or will she open a walkie-talkie channel and beg someone bigger and badder than herself to call the shots?

The bartender's eyes glint with ill humour; she gestures with a bear's paw towards a fridge linked by a mass of wires to an open mains. It thrums with intermittent power, emitting sour odours.

I look round to see if anyone's laughing at me. Two women who on first appearance might be more at home in a library, all narrow sloping shoulders and owl-glass eyes, play pool quietly in a corner and don't look up.

"Okay, I get it," I say. "Pinktown has power as well as attitude. Bully for you."

Electric lights, tinny MP3 player, fridge... so much sound and light and heat. An army of farmers must be pedalling away in a factory nearby, turning muscle and movement into electricity. Unpaid and underage, probably.

But unless someone pays me to go and find out, it's probably not my concern.

The bartender suddenly checks her watch and her eyes widen; she cranks the handle on a wind-up radio and the sounds of a roller derby game crackle into life, popcorned with static. From the bloodlust roar of the crowd it sounds like someone's been wounded. I crane my ears to hear the voice of the commentator above the hissing radio surf.

"The pivot's down, folks. I repeat... the pivot is down. Plenty of blood on the dancefloor, and the swipe and wipe crew has scooted on to clean things up before the other gals slide around in it and call foul. But Miss Pink's given the okay sign, and don't she always, no matter how red it gets, and the pivot nods the okay too, and she's up on her feet again. Holding her arm, sure, but at least she's still got her feet. Maybe this time the Hellcats'll get their lead jammer in play. C'mon, Hellcats! Make a play!"

The bartender nods in satisfaction and then the radio sputters to a stop, wound down to silence once more. If I left the bartender to it, she'd be cranking that handle all day. I want her to focus on me, not the game.

"Look. Never mind the white stuff. How's the water?"

Only specific London enclaves serve treats like Red Stripe and Irn Bru, but *all* enclave bars serve H2O. Brackish? Irradiated? Tasting of plastic? You can order any kind you like, honey. And almost certainly a few you don't.

"It ain't fresh, and it ain't cold." The bartender shrugs. "Reckon it costs a little more than you can afford..."

She slings a judicious eye over my old desert boots, protective leathers and scuffed backpack. Cornrowed hair that's seen brighter colours and skin that's seen better days. People look at me and see a road rat hopping from one enclave to another to seek their fortune. A wary but ultimately stupid little solo traveller, pitifully unaware that if you want to survive in post-plague London you have to buckle up and pick a team.

Well, I *picked* a team, thanks. Team Solo. With London divided by territorial enclave manifestos soaked with blood the moment they were drawn up, a wetjob is often performed better by a single sneakthief than an entire army.

But it has to be the right person. And, for a price, that's who I'm willing to be. Today I'll see a road rat in the mirror. With a little preparation, tomorrow I might see an exotic flesh girl, a raw-skinned beggar, a wasteland doctor or an old man. If I were to stare directly into my eyes, however... I'd see a loner with a secret, a growing bank account and a plan.

Beyond the sewers of Pinktown lies the Thames, see, and moored there is *My Way,* a ship just one down payment away from having a new captain. A single wetjob separates me from a stinking walk, a final payout and freedom. Fuck the enclaves, fuck people, and fuck the plague and its little dog too.

My ship, honey. My rules.

I just... can't... wait.

I pull out my wallet, bursting at the seams with beads, drugs, salt, flash drives, gold coins, condoms; enclave currency in all denominations. Road rats aren't known for their wealth, but I needn't maintain my cover now I've penetrated Pinktown. Now I need to be someone dangerous. Special. Worth being given a place on the team.

What happens next is my audition.

"Just water, then. Mug. Unchipped if you've got it."

"Fussy," sniffs the bartender.

I flash my cash as I pay, ensuring the bartender gets a good look at my concentrated wealth. Then I ever-so-hastily stuff the wallet back into my backpack, marvelling at how quickly the bartender's eyes turn into gold coins.

It's funny, isn't it? How desperate we are, even in adverse circumstances, to mould ourselves into stories worth telling? Europe may have become a piss-heap since the oil-plague. Fertility may be down, Tampax and Mooncups a luxury more likely to appear in fevered dreams than reality. Beggars may be starving in the streets, so emaciated that when you shudder and think "dead man walking" you realise it could be any gender standing ruined before your averted eyes... but in all this misery, some part of the human race *still* buys into the glamorous dream of the celluloid Wild West.

The Apocalypse? It's just uncharted territory, hon, waiting to be populated with heroes and villains and given meaning on the big screen. The new frontier with evocative SFX and a sepia filter. So let's count up our wagons and head out yonder, turning our profile to the camera like the professionals we are...

And now I'm the star of the show, drawing interest from all sides. The narrow-shouldered librarians I spotted earlier break off their game of pool and stand wary and expectant. One of them licks their lips. The room darkens as I hear a door being closed softly behind me.

I'd say there are three women behind me and the bartender in front.

Not enough.

The bartender is first to move. She grabs for the backpack containing the wallet but I swing it off the counter and follow through with a roundhouse thrust into her face; the backpack has got some heavy shit in it and I hear the sound of crunching cartilage. A broken nose? If so, I feel for her. I know *that* one.

The librarians are next. They're working tag-team. One sidles round to kneel behind me in ambush while the other lances forward with her pool cue in an attempt to topple me over the one lying in wait behind. So slow, these girls. So very slow.

I spend much of my downtime handcrafting mnemonics, hardwiring my synapses with a potent home brew of Cognitive-Behavioural Therapy. Alchemising the un/sub/conscious is my hobby; with no TV and no-one to trust and no kitchen to bake cupcakes in there's fuck all else to do. All it takes is a finger to a pressure point on the neck and I'm briefly flooded with adrenaline, reflexes heightened so that time warps and slows like a traffic accident. I used to be a courier. I've been in an accident or two, motorbike slung into a curve it can't handle. I know what the time does.

I jump onto the kneeling girl's back, guide the jabbing pool cue right past me into the soft bits of the bartender who's slowly getting to her feet, and slam a tiger palm into the librarian who's still standing.

And then, all of a sudden, she isn't. I'm not surprised. I have strong palms.

Only one of them left. I jump off my perch, careful to avoid the thick owl-eye spectacles fallen to the ground. I haven't seen an optician open to trade since pre-plague and stamping on those frail plastic frames would effectively render their wearer blind.

I fling my backpack at a slender-looking woman in leathers. It's a netball throw, a forward thrust from the chest. If you've got a mindset like mine, most sports are martial arts in disguise. I always did love netball.

She's quick, the one in leathers, but not quick enough; the backpack and its contents slam her in the chest with an audible *whuff.*

I've passed my audition. The prone bartender finally opens a channel and talks into her walkie-talkie in a soft voice.

And the response team hits the bar fast. By the time I've turned round I see four women in front of me, and for all their heavy kit I didn't even hear them enter. Only four, but they're professionals. Body armour, visors, batons, tasers and at least one visible gun. Even though the pink miniskirts above the spiked kneepads provide a disconcerting contrast, I know what I'm looking at. I've finally drawn the attention of someone at the top.

And as the security guards empty my backpack onto the floor with a metal clang, we all stare at the only thing in there apart from my wallet...

Polished. Buffed. Needle-sharp.

A pair of rollerblades.


I come to with a throbbing head that feels twice its normal size. I try blinking but it's a no-go: one eye is puffed and shut. The guards did a professional job on me: no bones broken, but my entire body is nonetheless mapped with cities and rivers of pain.

I'm bound to a chair in a concrete room with one door, no windows. It has the feeling of *underground.* Metal lockers surround me on all sides. A changing room?

A distant roar comes from somewhere beyond the door. At first I think it's the drumming throb of illicit machinery. Then I realise it's the sound of the crowd.

Slouched before me on chairs are five women, one of whom cradles a bloody arm. Shaved hair, dyed hair, mouse-brown hair, afro and grey... they all sport diverse plumage, but that's completely beside the point. What matters is the tight pink shorts, the protective pads on elbows and knees, the t-shirts bearing the same logo of a heavy pink paw with long claws. What matters is the helmets cradled lovingly in arms or slung on the backs of chairs. And the rollerblades that I've heard these women never take off, not even for bathing or screwing. Used to be skates, I've heard. Not any more.

I'm looking at the Pinktown Hellcats, number two extreme roller derby team in London. With all that money and training piled into them they might even become number one. That's probably why the jammer for the number one team, West Hammerettes, assigned the hit on the target sitting before me, distinguishable by the stars on her helmet.

And towering over them, all naked seven feet of her, is the team coach and the enclave's matriarch leader. Filaments course beneath Miss Pink's skin, giving weight to prior intel for which I paid a heavy price: *Don't look, don't touch,* they said. *Miss Pink's been modded. It's not sweat she secretes. Her entire body is poison.*

"Okay," I say, looking up. And up. Until I'm finally staring her in the eyes. "You got me. I confess... I didn't expect you to be buck-naked."

Best not to mention knowledge of her biotoxins, perhaps. When you're tied to a chair, there's no point in giving a person ideas.

"Interesting. You expected to see me at all?" Miss Pink's voice is dry, somewhere between cut glass and desert sand. She arches the area that used to be her eyebrow before she shaved them both off. She is quite hairless in her nudity, a giant lethal baby mouse. A poor analogy, of course: I see little vulnerability here. But baby mice are one of the few things as naked as her.

"Most road rats passing through here make considerable effort to avoid registering on my radar. Which begs the question: *Why* have you made me take an interest? *What* do you hope to gain?" Miss Pink clearly picks up on the little things. My brain feels bruised on the inside. I need to get her off-track.

"I came here to see *you,* of course. But... naked?"

Miss Pink sighs. "A film I liked. Molly Ringwald attends the dance in a pink dress she makes herself, a finger poked in society's collective eye. The original ending was that she turns up naked. *Pretty in Pink*. You see?"

"Okay," I reply. "Unclothed 24/7? Subversive. A more permanent statement than a business tie or a band t-shirt. I get that. Another question before you kill me, though. Pinktown? You're one of the toughest matriarchies in London. Isn't pink rather... soft?"

At this, the women seated before me burst into ribald laughter. It comes at me in a gale, threatening to blow me and my chair to the floor.

"You're entertaining thoughts of pre-pubescent youth? Of ribbons and frocks and icing?" The naked giantess smiles tightly.

"You are seriously fucking mistaken, my dear. Pink is as soft as... organs. The pulpy bits that give life and take it away. Blood and eternity. The red and the white. You're not the first to mistake what lies beneath the colour pink. Many have done so."

The leader stretches out her gums in a smile so predatory I can see past her incisors to her molars. "Then again, many have died."

The women seated on the chairs shuffle slightly and I read their body language like a sailor eyes a clear sky and sniffs a storm. I notice, then, their weapons: a knife, a bowling ball, spiked knuckles, a power glove, something I thought was a cigarillo tucked behind the ear but now recognise to be a blowpipe. Though I don't see the darts, they won't be far from that one's hand.

"Miss Pink?" The Hellcat with the grey hair casts a sidelong glance at the door. "Half-time's over. They're calling for us. The game, it's..."

Miss Pink sniffs, a short puff of irritation.

"Be silent, little one. I *am* the game."

She turns back to me. If she's a giant baby mouse then I'm a tiny cat, and she's eyeing me as if she's intrigued to see how far I can get away before she pounces. In another situation I might fancy my chances, but from everything I've seen and heard of Miss Pink she's here to control games, not indulge in them. She's willing to interrogate me in the middle of a bout, after all. She must have a policy of dealing with troublemakers as soon as possible.

"Give me a reason why you shouldn't die, my dear." The tones of the giantess are affable, at odds with her narrowed eyes. "We're halfway through a game, as the good lady said, and I don't want to have to deal with you. You display an inconvenient streak of rebellion. And more money than a road rat should possess.

And no allegiance to me, which is a concern. I have both a team and an enclave to run, dear. I have precious little time to waste on concern."

"I saved up for safe passage across London. I'm here to join the Hellcats." I keep my voice low, humble. All part of the plan. "You may be number two in the league tables, but only someone stupid would fail to recognise you're the best."

"And you're *not* stupid, my dear? My. We *have* been blessed with your fortuitous arrival." It's a silky challenge, sweetness belying threat. Challenges must be faced.

"Listen. I took out four women in your bar, remember? I crossed London on my own steam."

I pause. "*And* I have blades."

I've done my research. "You lost your last bout against the West Hammerettes. You lose *every* bout you play against them. Maybe... I'm just what you need."

I stare at the Hellcats in turn. The jammer with the mouse-brown hair, my designated target. Currently so strong and full of life, but now she's just a box in the ground waiting to happen. I never said I earned my money cleanly. The plague has robbed us all, stealing things we can never buy back.

The jammer repays my gaze with a bold, almost hungry look. The others stare at me with resentment, apprehension, contempt. The usual things. The expected things.

"What do *you* think, dear?" Miss Pink's question is directed at the jammer.

"I think –"

Miss Pink's smile silences her as quickly as a laugh. "I was joking, dear one. I pay. I feed. I clothe. *I* choose. And this road rat seems nasty. Quick too, from what I've heard about the incident in the bar. We'll take her."

"Miss, shouldn't she... be tested, at least?" The pivot with the dyed hair and the striped helmet cover sounds hesitant, but at least she's brave enough to speak: I find myself silently cheering her on. "We've jammed everyone from the Hoxton Merkins to the Edgeware Wolves into the ground. Aren't we already the best? She *needs* testing."

Interesting. Her weapon is the bowling ball, and she looks strong enough to use it. She'd have made a great blocker, but to be the team's pivot she must have an edge. Speed. Appearances can deceive; one to watch. And she looks the least pleased to see me. The glances she casts at the jammer are protective and, I think, more than that. She's defending the jammer's good name with the tenacity of not only a crew member but a lover.

The jammer turns pale at the pivot's intervention and her lips twitch. It's a warning glance she casts at her girlfriend, her pivot, her ally. I've used it myself on an ex-boyfriend struggling in the dock for drug-related crimes he didn't commit. Well, okay, he did. *Shut up,* it says. *I love you, but you need to shut the fuck up.*

Miss Pink muses, stroking her smooth chin. "The little fool has bought her own blades," she says finally. "Rosetta? You're wounded, I see. When I specifically asked you to take a little more care."

The pivot, Rosetta, blanches.

"A scratch, Miss," she says hastily. She's the one who was cradling her bloody arm earlier. On closer inspection I can see it's not just a superficial cut; her arm's serrated down to the bone. Blood coagulates on the floor in a pool. Hacksaw damage, I'd say. I hear the blood-lust in the crowd somewhere above and beyond. The pivot needs serious medical attention, and this bout is only at half-time. Bouts last longer than they used to. Now they can last anywhere between an hour and a lifetime.

Miss Pink steps forward and strokes the pivot's bare face with a naked hand.

"Good night, dear." Her voice is unexpectedly soft. The girl with the striped helmet clutches her throat as biotoxins enter her system, jackknifes at the knees and dies.

I hear the whisper of unease among the team, yet nothing is said. I don't quite understand. I mean, I don't mind killing people for *money.* When it comes to what should and shouldn't be, people create their own subjective rules and argue 'til they're blue in the face about why those opinions are not subjective at all. That's what the internet turned into. I remember the internet.

But this death is… unclean. This was the team's pivot. The jammer's girlfriend. No money changed hands. A woman stroked another woman's face, and that woman died.

Yet nothing is even *said?*

"Congratulations. You're the new pivot. Feeling proud?"

Miss Pink points to the slumped body. "She was Rosetta Stoned. The only name that matters. For reasons of convenience you'll also be known as Rosetta Stoned. I see your blades are too small. As are hers." She nudges the cooling pile of meat, the remains of someone whose real name I'll never know.

"We'll find you replacements. In the meantime, Poison Ivy will take the dead girl's blades and give you hers."

One of the blockers (grey hair, power glove) turns to the leader of Pinktown in horror.

"I haven't taken these blades off in five *years...*"

"You like having feet?" Miss Pink eyes the blocker coolly. "Feet are worth keeping, I hear. Take off your rollerblades."

With something approaching a strangled sob, the grey-haired blocker, Poison Ivy, removes her blades with shaking hands. Making a valiant and successful attempt not to throw them at my face, she places them carefully and neatly before me.

None of us look at her. This is a violation. It's not something anyone would want to see.


And that's how I become the Hellcats' pivot on a probationary basis: halfway into a bout, sporting unfamiliar blades seamed with another woman's sweat. As we leave Rosetta's body on the floor and head towards the arena, I study the reactions of the others and am disheartened by what I see. Their expressions are bitter and drawn; they keep their eyes averted. No-one speaks, and the death of the pivot goes carefully unremarked as we head through a narrow corridor leading from the locker room towards a closed door vibrating with the stamping of feet in the arena beyond.

Spurred on by the roaring approval of a full crowd, hampered by our poor technique and the Hellcat's mistrust of the new girl, we win the bout. But only just.

The problem is that tactics are assigned not by the team, but by Miss Pink as she smiles thinly into the crowd, her thumb held high or low like a Roman emperor. And it's clear she doesn't know *shit* about team tactics. Already I can see the only things she understands are money, power and death.


In the days that follow I keep looking for an opportunity to terminate my target, but something holds me back. Professionalism, I hope. These team members do everything together, enveloping me into their bawdy activities with an endearing lack of formality, and I just can't get the jammer on her own, the way I'd prefer. I need a smooth kill and a clean getaway before the final bout of the season; I'd be doing my client a favour.

My delay is, I promise myself, absolutely nothing to do with a growing thawing of intentions, or a budding affection for this sport and this team.

Weeks of training... do some good, I think. They soften the Hellcats' initial hatred of me. They were right to hate me. My arrival killed their friend. But shared sweat can help to build a bond, fragile though it may be. While loving men, I've always preferred the company of women, but never felt a part of their group. Always different, isolated. Unique. In the wrong way.

It seems different, here. We sweat, we fight, we guffaw. We begin to tell each other secrets. We... unify. And every time we hit the track, I do my best to prove that I've dropped my attitude along with my road rat leathers.

Skating in Rosetta's old bloodstained things while I wait to be officially assigned kit, the somehow comforting smell of iron lingering in her inherited protective pads, I do whatever the Hellcats say. I can't wear my own set of their colours until they say so, and that's fine by me. I listen to their commands. I play by their rules. As pivot, I don't fight to control the rink. I don't yearn to be number one. We're all there for the jammer, and she's there for us. We're together, the Hellcats, a Portuguese Man of War, a colonial organism of many entities moving and thinking as one. That's how it works.

And after a few weeks I discover I like them. I trust them. And, I think, they trust me.

I learn their names: the mousey jammer is Vicky Vitriol. Poison Ivy, the grey-haired blocker with the power glove, has just about forgiven me for wearing her blades. The blocker with the afro hair and the switchblade is Dirty Martini, and I nearly leap on her with delight the day she reveals she's spent her month's savings on a bottle of Kahlua. There's always fresh milk and vodka for our White Russians, of course. We're stars. And the shaven-skulled blocker with the blow-pipe that never leaves its spot by her ear? That's Typhoid Mary. She found her way into the Hellcats because the rest of the world only ever saw half-woman, half-birthmark. We see *her*.

We.

One evening, Dirty Martini fingers my cornrows as we slip away for White Russians on the rooftops of an old car park.

"What's your name? Your real one? Not the one that..." she leaves the rest unsaid, and the face of the woman whose name I inherited hangs between us in the air.

"Nabirye," I say. "Yours?"

"Masani," she says. We laugh, leaving the obvious unspoken: we knew we were both of Ugandan descent the minute we laid eyes on each other.

"You know, Vicky's wound up pretty tight," I say. Probing. Gathering information.

A shadow passes over Masani's eyes. "We're Miss Pink's pets," she eventually replies. "Celebrity pets on golden chains. Fed, watered, sold, executed. All on a whim. It gets to Vicky. I see her standing on this roof alone, sometimes. I'm worried she might…"

And that night, when I pull a concealed lockpick from my cornrows and rifle through Vicky Vitriol's locker to find a plastique gun that must have cost her a year's wages, I take it. I know how to use it better than she does.

She's cracked. Snapped. Broken.

By hook or by crook, that girl wants *out.*

And I can help her with that. It's my job.


We're assembled in the locker room with ten minutes to go before our biggest bout as a new line-up. We're up against the West Hammerettes, of course, but what my cherished Hellcats don't know is that it doesn't matter now.

"Okay, you're now officially a Hellcat." Vicky sounds terse but shrill above the drumming of the crowd. No mention of things missing from her locker. "Here. Your colours. You've earned them. Strip."

She thrusts a T-shirt and pink shorts at me, and the crowbar I asked for as my own personal weapon – and that's when I finally realise that, beneath their tiny pink shorts, the Hellcats go commando.

Damn.

There's nothing for it. I pull off my vest, leggings and genital modesty straps and, buck-naked, accept the inevitable stares.

Vicky's eyes go round and wide as she stares at my vagina.

And, just above it, my penis.

My resplendent penis. And vagina.

I like to think I have glorious examples of both.

"You're… intersex?" she whispers.

"Yeah," I say, somewhat surprised she steered clear of "hermaphrodite," a term which, to me, smacks of the freakshow.

"But... Pinktown and the Hellcats practise segregation. No men allowed."

I tense, but only a little. My fault. No time for diplomacy. I should have expected this. "Working ovaries. No gonads. I think of myself as an intersex woman. I tell you this... I'm definitely not a man."

There's a pause.

"Oh, fuck it," says Vicky, and she pumps the air with a fist. "Get to it, Hellcats. Let's GO!"

The roar of the crowd is deafening. Bowing to Miss Pink, sedate and alone in what might as well be a royal balcony fuzzed with an anti-metal energy barrier, we take our places on the pivot line. I look round to the jammer line thirty yards behind to see Vicky staring at me intently.

Across the track, the Hammerettes in their blue-and-wine bikinis shake tasers at us and laugh. Tasers? Of *course* we – I mean, the Hellcats – never win. Their jammer gives me a knowing wink and nods meaningfully at Vicky Vitriol. My target. My ally.

And tucked into my helmet is a small plastique gun.

Play starts. We do okay at first, walling up nicely and whipping Vicky round so she's off like a rocket. It quickly turns into an ugly version of *Wacky Races* with spiked elbow pads and fists and blood flying and big cartoon bubbles saying POW and ZAP and BOOM. But the Hammerettes earn lead jammer, and it's all we can do to steer clear of their tasers, and then, ignoring the boos of the crowd, we start to lose, lose, lose.

Fuck them. A real roller derby crowd would never boo. These people are here for the blood and spilled entrails, not the sheer mad joy of it.

Fuck them all and their little dog too.

I stretch out a languid arm and everyone stares at the little plastique gun in my hand. The Hammerettes position themselves into a Death Wall, but their jammer stops them: she thinks the gun's aimed at Vicky. I can see it in her eyes: *about time.*

I'm one bullet away from my final downpayment and a ship. Freedom.

Freedom... to do *what*, exactly?

I fire. A tiny plastique bullet passes through a fuzzy energy barrier, and Miss Pink's face explodes in a dainty crimson rosette.

I think it looks beautiful.

Gameplay stops, and Vicky turns to me. "You killed Miss Pink," she whispers. "The leader of Pinktown."

"Nah," I say. "I don't care about that. I killed your coach."

The silent crowd pauses, time slowing like a traffic accident, then rises to its feet in a roar of approval. It's had the blood it came for. Any blood will do.

I don't know what will happen next... but who ever does?

"Listen up to your new coach," I tell the team. "I've got a way we can deal with those tasers, see. Watch *this*."

We skate towards the Hammerettes in a new formation, often talked about in the locker room but never approved by Miss Pink and put into practice, and for the first time what I see on their faces is fear, even as security guards gather round the track like pink-skirted vultures.

We're a team at last, freed at last from enclaves and bullshit and fear. Even if it's only until the end of this bout.

But time slows, like a traffic accident. Time is on our side, and so is the blood-thump, foot-stomp, baying, screaming crowd.

And we'll make it out of here alive. I know we will.

Because dead girls don't wear blades.

**Gavin Inglis**

The invitation arrived in a black-bordered, skull-print envelope. It was marked 'Transatlantic Traction Fund' and contained thirteen free plane tickets, from Glasgow to Chicago.

Iona Uzi peered at it with one eye closed. They had been on a cider binge with the Sheffield Slayers the night before. The offer didn't surprise her; her team had won the Birmingham Blitz and roller derby was huge in the States. She only got the bad feeling much, much later. After they landed at Chicago O'Hare and she got the text saying last year's winners had never come home.

The hotel was plush, with a free cab service thrown in. They did the canal tour and the aquarium and trained in Grant Park, wind from the lake blasting in their faces. They bought stupid goth shit on Halsted and when Iona got back to the hotel there was a giant woman waiting to see her.

They took coffee in the bar. Iona clocked in at five foot ten, but this woman was *Guinness Book of Records* material. Her eyes sat deep in their sockets, and her hair was a pile of black with a white streak straight out of old Hammer horror movies. She held their biggest mug as if it were a thimble, and announced that the bout was on for the following afternoon at the New Coliseum. Glasses behind the bar rattled with every word she said.

"I started this fund back in the seventies. We like to give you Brits a taste of real roller derby."

"What's your team called?"

"Chicago Cadavers."

"Nice. And what should I call you?"

"I'm Big Shelley. See ya at the track."

The giant woman stooped at the door. She left a sticky, cloying scent behind her. It reminded Iona of decaying flowers.


"Holy shit," Mairi Murder said, as they entered the Coliseum.

"No blasphemy," said Sister Swedge. But she stared too, transfixed by the four-thousand-seater stadium and its custom track. Back home they played in sports centres on a track marked in blue tape. Here there was a rail, banks, lighting rigs and TV cameras. Technicians swarmed across them, testing the booms.

"Skates on, right now," said Iona. "Let's get the hang of these banks before the punters show up."

An hour later they did their entrance lap, posing for the TV cameras. Lights obscured the spectators, but a colossal roar greeted every skater. Jocasta Disaster did her Beyoncé wiggle. Mental Nicky gave the cameras the Johnny Cash finger.

The Chicago Cadavers entered, dressed in yellow. The volume level rose until the floor shook beneath their feet. The rival team slid round the track, fists raised, ignoring the Scots. Their movements were jerky, their skin pallid, hair dangling in ratty clumps.

"It's not exactly Beverly Hills 90210," Kirsty Karnage said.

"They're stiff as anything," Mental Nicky pounded her palm. "We'll skate right round them."

But when Iona saw Big Shelley standing in the shadows, arms folded, she got that bad feeling again.

The Chicago girls said nothing as they formed the pack. The home team had provided most of the referees, but Judy of Judgment was in place watching the Chicago jammer. The whistle blew and the pack moved into motion. Two more whistles and the jammers set off.

Immediately, Mental Nicky was in there, swooping past the pack to take lead jammer, her Adam Ant face stripe catching the light. She pounded around the track, head down, leaning into the corners and bearing down on the Chicago blockers. Swinging to the outside, she feinted and lunged, breaking through a gap to score, sliding past the pivot to hug the corner. She howled her happy hour howl, punching the air as a camera tracked her. Then she put her head back down and did it all again.

The Chicago jammer fumbled in the middle of the pack. Her blockers tried to clear a path while Mairi and Sister Swedge checked them. The pale Chicago pivot seemed in a trance, taking the curves like a sleepwalker, making no move to block. Nicky thundered past for a third lap and gave a banshee wail.

From the bench, Iona stared at the action. Something was wrong. Chicago were supposed to be champions. What the hell was going on? She watched Heather Havoc setting the pace, confused by how easy it was; Big Shelley, eyes glittering as she watched; and the Chicago jammer, going nowhere.

Then she noticed one of the referees biting through Judy of Judgment's skull.

The Scottish official had ceased to follow the action. Her legs gave way and her eyes rolled back as red blood deluged her black-and-white referee's stripes.

It seemed some to be sort of signal. The Chicago blockers converged on Mairi Murder, grabbing at her spiderweb armwarmers. Their jammer slowed, watching the track for Nicky's next approach. The Chicago pivot turned to Heather Havoc and clawed at the Scottish pivot's face.

"Fuck," said Iona.

The jam disintegrated. Heather tumbled over the rail, her teeth gritted as she wrestled the slavering undead pivot. Nicky squared up to the jammer and shouldered her aside. Dead tendons strained to catch their balance on the skates. But Mairi was in big trouble, caught from both sides as a third blocker tore at the back of her vest.

The crowd gave a rumble of disapproval. Iona, with sudden, perfect clarity, saw what she had to do.

Ducking beneath the rail, behind the pack, she skated directly at the guzzling referee. A quick glance into Judy's half-empty brain cavity told her that particular struggle was over. Iona grabbed the whistle which hung on a cord around the Chicago referee's neck, and yanked it. The cord sliced easily through the greedy zombie's flesh. Her ragged head toppled to the floor.

Mairi was on her knees now, forced to the ground, the third blocker lined up for a killing blow. Iona took a deep breath and blew the whistle as loud as she could.

Immediately, the Chicago team froze, turning their withered faces to the centre zone. The audience hushed. Iona felt four thousand faces staring at her. She took another deep breath and pointed to Mairi.

"Block to the back!" she yelled. "Forcing a skater down – major penalty!"

Nobody moved. Sweat trickled down Iona's neck. Then a murmur of agreement rose from the audience. The offending undead slumped and trudged off to the penalty box.

Iona skated to her team. "You OK?"

"Let's get the fuck out of here!" Terminal Felicity was one of their new blockers. Her eyes were wide and her body was shaking.

"Language," said Sister Swedge.

"Get it together," Iona hissed. "There are four thousand of them watching." A TV camera dipped close. She noticed for the first time that it was crewed by a grinning skeleton. "We won't make it out of the building. We have to win this. Understand?" She gripped Felicity's hand. "We took down London. The undead should be a piece of piss."

Heather Havoc staggered back to the rail, listing visibly to one side. Behind her, body parts littered the ground in a trail of slime. She tried to step back onto the track, wobbled and crashed to the floor.

"Give us her helmet cover," Iona said. "I'll take pivot."

They formed the pack once more, bunched up against the Chicago blockers as the jam began. One stared at Mairi with hungry dead eyes. She thrust an elbow into the corpse's ribs. It made a wet, sticky sound. A decaying referee skated close.

"Stick to the rules. We have to win over the crowd." Iona made a space for Nicky to pass but this time the Chicago jammer cut through, skating in long, mechanical strides, sparks trailing from her skates. Nicky pounded in pursuit. Chicago equalised and their pivot called off the jam. They were playing pussy tactics.

"We need better blocking," spat Nicky.

"You try blocking something that's trying to eat your face!" Mairi Murder wailed.

"The problem," Sister gave the officials a stern look, "is that the referees aren't calling penalties on Chicago. They're grabbing, cutting the track, using the head…"

A new corpse eyed up Mairi as the next jam started. The Chicago jammer edged ahead with some dubious cornering. Mairi used a forearm to keep the drooling blocker away. Immediately a judge blew a penalty against the Scottish team.

"I've had it," said Nicky, and swung off the track. She rammed a shoulder into the referee's face as she passed, and knocked his entire lower jaw off. Confused, he attempted to wedge the whistle back into the vacant space. It dropped to the floor.

"Legal block," said Nicky.

The Chicago girls were getting nasty now, tearing at the visitors' strips, clashing yellowed teeth against battered helmets. The new pivot raked Iona's neck with long, dirty nails. The audience seemed strangely quiet.

"No team from England's gonna beat us," hollered Big Shelley.

"That might be true …" said Iona. The rival pivot leered close, licking its withered lips. Iona smacked her right in the kisser. Dry bones cracked. "… but we're not from England!"

The Scots swung to the attack, grappling and pounding as they skated. Terminal Felicity tore off an arm. Mairi Murder went for the knees. Mental Nicky knocked a blocker right over the rail. And Sister Swedge lifted her crucifix, intoned a brief prayer, and thrust it straight into the Chicago jammer's cranial cavity.

The track piled up with debris: fractured bones, spattered organs and sticky fluids of uncertain origin. Hesitant at first, then with growing conviction, the audience began to cheer the visitors.

Iona saluted the cameras. But as they passed the Chicago bench, she saw Big Shelley strapping on a pair of skates, each as big as Iona's first car. The hall grew quiet as the manager stepped over the rail. The track creaked beneath her. From the jammer line, Big Shelley began to skate, her massive thighs pumping like industrial compressors.

"Crap," said Nicky. "It's the end of level boss."

"Skate!" shouted Iona.

They ground the track, Shelley gaining on them like a Tyrannosaurus Rex. Mairi stumbled, but Sister grabbed her and pulled her upright. Big Shelley slid closer. Up front, Nicky desperately signalled for the end of the jam. "Worth a shot," she shrugged.

"You girls think you're so hip, with your monster mash make-up and your flat tracks!" Shelley spat. "I was there at the Transcontinental! I was there at the Hippodrome! I skated Madison Square Gardens!"

"What is she talking about?" Felicity gasped.

Shelley was panting like a perv on a PA system. Her shadow fell across them.

"You love roller derby," she snarled. "But you weren't there in '73 when they shut it down. My team was breaking up. All the stars were moving on. Somebody needed to keep it alive. To preserve the skills for the future. For you girls! All it took was some special embalming fluid. And one little bus crash."

Big Shelley stopped and turned around. Momentum carried the Scots on, round the corner, directly towards her. "Do we break off?" called Nicky. Iona shook her head.

"You've got to pay your dues, girls," Shelley grinned and flexed vice-like hands. "I need fresh bodies every year to keep my team going. Fit bodies. Skilled bodies. Come to Momma!"

"Your roller derby," Iona yelled. "It was staged. Jumps and dives and set pieces. It was worse than the wrestling."

"We were no phonies!"

"Fake," yelled Iona. "Fake, fake, fake."

Shelley screamed and charged at the oncoming skaters, lips drawn back, exposing the blackened, ragged stumps of her ancient teeth.

Iona hung back and stretched her arms out to the blockers.

"Okay guys," she said. "Whip it."

Mairi and Felicity grabbed her and twisted their hips in perfect unison. Iona shot forward, cannonballing towards this gargantuan Bride of Frankenstein on rollerskates. "We're the future!" she hissed. "Get off the track."

And Iona leapt, shielding her face with her arms. There was a rubbery impact, a brief, sickening, squelch, then she was lying on the track wrapped in Big Shelley's internal organs. The immense husk tottered, stared down at the hole in its chest, and finally toppled, taking out a TV camera and a twenty-foot section of rail.

A deafening roar split the Coliseum as the pack swept through, gathering up Iona. On their victory lap she saw the audience at last, on their feet in faded uniforms, and she understood who they had been playing to all this time. Four thousand long-dead rollergirls cheered them on; energised, revitalised, punching the air. The Chicago scene was about to get a whole lot bigger.

The Scots took a second lap, then a third, and now the crowd were shouting one word together.

"Re-match! Re-match! Re-match!"

"Whaddya think?" said Mental Nicky.

"Fuck that," said Iona. "Head for the airport."

**Daphne Du Gorier**

Detective Morten took a swig of his coffee as he waited for his deputy's report. It tasted like rocket fuel, but he had a feeling he'd need every drop to get him through the night. A storm had hung in the muggy air for days and now a few drops fell, landing on the dusty concrete of the alley floor and mingling with the oil and dirt. They'd need a tent to prevent the crime scene being contaminated.

"Forensics will be here soon, sir."

Morten took one last gulp of his coffee, tipping the cooling styrofoam cup upwards to swallow the dregs, before addressing his deputy. "Neighbours see anything?"

"No, sir."

"You took statements and questioned them ?"

"Yes, sir. There were no signs they were withholding information."

The inspector released a harsh breath. "This isn't looking good." He addressed his deputy, the words unpleasant on his tongue. "You know what we have to do, don't you?"

"H-him, sir?"

"What option do we have? We're coming up empty. We need him."

"I understand, sir. I'll make the call."

The day-long tournament had drawn a good crowd. They'd spent the break stocking up on food and drink and discussing the high points so far. Further down from the refreshment stand, tables full of merchandise had done a bustling trade, selling everything from branded t-shirts to bumper stickers. Photographers snapped shots of rollergirls in mid-air as they warmed up on the track. Over the speakers, an announcer gave the crowd their two-minute warning. It was nearly time for the next bout.

"It wasn't a major!" Gemma Jukes was five foot two, wearing a bright orange uniform, sweaty and scowling. She was terrifying. And she was determined to have her say about a penalty from the last bout.

"Your forearms made contact with the opposing blocker," Vanessa Vanquish, first-time NSO, pointed out. The official wished she'd been quick enough to avoid ambush. Unfortunately, wheels gave the skaters a significant speed advantage.

"Are you blind?" Gemma raised her eyebrows. "They were nowhere near touching!"

"That's not what the ref saw."

"Then he needs to get his eyes checked!"

Vanessa could feel sweat beading on the back of her neck and a glance at the clock informed her that if she wasn't on track in less than thirty seconds, there'd be hell to pay. "I'm just repeating what the ref told me."

"It wasn't a major!"

"It was a major" another voice cut in. "Look at your wristguards."

Scowling, Gemma presented her wrists to the newcomer. "What about them?"

The man – a referee with a black-and-white striped shirt and whistle hanging from his neck – gestured to the wristguards. Like many skaters, Gemma had used heavy-duty white tape to secure the straps and prevent any loose velcro becoming a safety hazard. The tape on the right guard was scuffed, but the left was smudged with black ink. "That's ink from her number. The only way it could have got there was when you hit her shoulder with your forearms. It was definitely a major."

Gemma gaped as if considering argument, before muttering an apology and leaving. Vanessa rubbed her brow with the back of her hand, making her fringe stick up with sweat.

"Thanks for that, Ripper." She glanced at the busy track behind him where two teams were lining up. "It's hard to be strict when they corner you. I wish I had your poker face, you never give out! I signed up to NSO at Rollercon this year and I'm dreading it already. What was I thinking?"

"You'll be fine. Rules are rules," Ripper said with a smile. "We have to uphold them, even when it's a pain."

"Tell me about it." Vanessa sighed. "I'd better get back. Hey," she noticed an odd, almost worried expression had crossed Ripper's face. "You okay?"

Ripper brushed away her concern with a wan smile. "It's nothing. I just had a bad feeling for a moment. It's probably – "

"Are you Potomac Ripper?" He was interrupted by one of the venue's management team marching towards them.

"That's me."

"There's a phone call for you at reception. They say it's urgent."


He didn't want to take the case. The police were a nightmare – if Ripper had wanted to spend his time fighting through red tape, he'd have joined the force in the first place.

Yet somehow he found himself at the address, ducking under the police tape and approaching Detective Morten. There had been something in the detective's voice when he'd requested Ripper. The police didn't like involving him, but he knew this city like they didn't. If they were calling him, there had to be a reason.

A makeshift gazebo provided some cover. Ripper walked towards it, rainwater running off his long jacket. It was a one-of-a kind with its vertical black-and-white stripes, and it had been through a lot more than rain.

As he ducked into the tent, his eyes were drawn past the people studying the crime scene to the body in the corner. The forensics team were moving around the inner cordoned area. Two more knelt near to the body, taking instruments out of a swab sample kit.

"Ripper, thanks for coming." Detective Morton appeared, shadowed by his deputy. He sounded anything but grateful.

"What's the situation?"

"Body was found four hours ago." Morton jerked his thumb towards the corpse. "No identification, no signs of a struggle and no witnesses. Forensic are sweeping the scene but so far they don't have any leads." He sighed. "It'll be a few days before the samples are processed, of course."

Ripper nodded, mentally taking note of this information, or lack thereof. "Mind if I examine the body?"

Morten glanced at the scene manager who was using a laptop to send images to the lab. "I can get you five minutes. No more than that."

"That's all I need," Ripper said, already moving.

He knelt a few feet away from the body. The scent of ripe garbage mixed with the sharp tang of blood. The corpse lay on his back: male and middle-aged. Hair cropped short and the beginning of wrinkles across a wide forehead. He was wearing a t-shirt, long shorts and socks, but no shoes. Ripper noted that the soles of the socks were free from any tell-tale marks, though the heels had a few smudges.

"We didn't find any shoes." Morten had been watching his assessment. "Could be any number of reasons. Maybe they could have been used to identify his assailant."

"You're sure this was an attack?"

"Looks like a blow to the head." He gestured to a dark purple bruise that blossomed from beneath the hairline. It was red and swollen at the centre. "We won't know for sure until we do a post-mort."

Ripper nodded, shifting to study the way the body had been laid. "Looks like he was dumped here."

"We found tyre-marks at the entrance to the alley, then there are tracks leading over here. Seems he was dragged part of the way."The scene manager approached them, a clipboard under his arm. "We've taken all the information. All the photos have been sent back to the lab, so the body can be transported."

With a nod, Morten beckoned to his crew, and they began loading the body onto a stretcher. Ripper watched, mulling ideas over in his head, then stepped forward, hoping to get a clearer look at the victim's face. He noted nothing of interest, and was about to move away. But then something caught his eye.

"Wait."

They hesitated, looking at Morten for direction, and he held up a hand. "What is it, Ripper?"

Ripper tore his eyes away from the design on the t-shirt, shaking his head.

"No...nothing. Just looking at his clothes."

Morten looked too, seeing the white t-shirt, muddy from he floor. "'Capital

City Slayers'," he read. "Do you think there's something there? Are they a local group? A band?"

"Must be." Ripper said, letting them take the body away. "Something like that." But his apprehension had amplified,

"Well?" Morten asked, as the door slammed shut and the engine rumbled into life. "What'll it be?"

"I'll take the case," Ripper said, hoping he didn't live to regret it. "Leave it to me."

Ripper spent some hours researching in his office. Dusk had fallen by the time he finally left and hailed a cab. Researching 'Capital City Slayers' online hadn't turned up much, but there had been a few mentions of a new roller derby league. There was nothing concrete. Or not yet, anyway. But if the police realised the logo on the shirt was more than a generic print, it'd mean trouble.

The DC rollergirls were Ripper's home league and the main league in the area, but a few months ago there had been whisperings of a break-away league. Given the natural rivalry for practice space, recruits and sponsorship between two leagues in one city, he hadn't expected to hear anything else until the new league was established. But Ripper had a sinking suspicion that he'd soon be finding out a lot more.

He had only one lead, so he had to take it. No matter how much he didn't want to.

Ripper hesitated for a moment before knocking on the door. A voice called from the inside, then the door eased open with a gentle creak.

"Ripper!" The girl standing in the open doorway gaped at him for a moment, a hand going to her tangled red hair and brushing it back from her face. "What are you doing here?"

He gave her an awkward half-smile, wishing he didn't have to lie. "Just wanted to catch up. Are you busy?"

"No, not at all. Come in!" She stepped back into the apartment, nearly tripping over an overflowing laundry basket as she retied her dressing gown over her pyjamas. She was wearing the pair with fried eggs printed all over them. If he hadn't seen them up close, he'd think they were flowers. Same old Scarlett.

Picking his path through the cluttered, but still familiar hallway, he crushed a pang of nostalgia, letting Scarlett lead him to battered leather armchair in the lounge.

"Do you want a drink? I'm out of coffee but I have a few herbal teas knocking around. Peppermint and raspberry, I think."

"Peppermint would be nice," Ripper said.

Scarlett nodded. "Right, you always… drink peppermint." She paused, pressing her lips together, then made an abortive gesture with her hands. "I'll put the kettle on."

While she was in the kitchen, Ripper scanned the room, noting Scarlett's bookshelves, arranged in colour order. Scarlett never cleaned or tidied. Not unless she was anxious.

She returned with the tea in a pretty blue teapot. "There's sugar, if you want."

"This is fine." He blew at the steam, watching her pour her own cup and sip from it. "How are things with you?"

"Good, just hectic." Her smile seemed the tiniest bit strained. But maybe he was trying to see something that wasn't there. "How are the rollers?"

"We're doing well. Just finished a big tournament." Ripper was relieved that she had brought up derby. It'd make his questioning seem more natural. "How about you? Did you set up your league yet?"

"Not yet." Scarlett shrugged. "There's so much to organise. Might be months before I manage to get anything solid."

"That's too bad," Ripper said. "I wanted to know if I could do anything to help. I could referee, or you could sell me a t-shirt. I'd be a walking advert."

"We're not at that stage yet. Besides, I'd hate to mess with your whole black-and-white thing." She gestured to his coat. "But thanks for the offer."

"Must be tough not skating," Ripper finished his tea, setting his cup back down. "How do you cope?"

"I've been doing a lot of running. Started a yoga class."

They chatted for a few minutes. Scarlett's answers didn't seem forced, but skating with her for three years had taught him a few things, and he knew she could stay calm under pressure. So Ripper couldn't draw any conclusions. He needed more evidence.

He asked if he could use the bathroom and Scarlett ushered him down the hall. He stepped inside trying to clear the thoughts being muddled by the sudden scents of perfume and shampoo filling the room. He needed to either verify that Scarlett was nothing to do with this, or invalidate her defence. A glance through her bathroom cabinet brought up nothing conclusive but Ripper's guilt at violating Scarlett's privacy. There was an open pack of painkillers, but they could have been for headaches, not derby bruising.

In the hallway he could hear running water: Scarlett was in the kitchen. Her bedroom door was closed. There could be a clue in there, but if Scarlett found him, he'd have no excuse. She knew about his work. She must already suspect that was why he was here. It'd only put her further on guard.

Still, he was getting nowhere by talking. So he inched the door open and peered inside.

It was dark, full of vague shapes and shadows. The bed and wardrobe, and then some lumps on the floor that could have been clothes or maybe more books. He took a deep breath as he scanned the room, then paused.

Beneath the normal smells of shampoo and laundry detergent, there was something else. Something distinctive.

But before he could analyse his discovery, he realised something else. The sound of running water had stopped. He quickly retreated back into the hallway, shutting the bedroom door as quietly as possible.

"I think I'm gonna head off," Ripper said as he entered the lounge to see Scarlett waiting for him. Her brow furrowed, but she nodded.

"Alright. It was nice to catch up."

Ripper managed to roll out some generic niceties as he left the apartment, but his mind was reeling. He had realised with a shock what the odour was. Padstink.

And that could only mean one thing. Scarlett was lying to him. And he had a horrible feeling he knew why.


It was time to take the investigation to the next level. He was certain the crime was connected to Scarlett's league – why else would she have been so cagey? Even if she denied its existence, he knew they'd been skating. And that meant they must have left tracks. For a league to practice, they needed a venue. And suitable skating venues were few and far between. They couldn't be in Dulles Sportsplex or Temple Hills; the DC rollergirls used those venues and the crossover would've been noticed. Plus the distance to those venues had been a factor in Scarlett wanting to start a new league. So if she'd done it, it'd make sense for it to be somewhere closer to home. Or at least on her side of the river.

On his computer, Ripper pulled up a map of the city, then marked Scarlet's apartment. Then he searched for nearby sports centres and skating rinks and noted their numbers. He spent a few hours making calls, but got no bites. Most people had no idea about roller derby. More than once, he found conversations that should have lasted minutes lagging for almost an hour, as he got carried away explaining.

Back on the map, Ripper contemplated it for a few moments before marking the location where the body had been found. It was on the same side of the river as Scarlet's apartment, but not too close. Scarlett didn't have a car, so assuming she was involved, wherever she was skating had to be close to home. Ripper drew a mile-wide circle around where the body had been found. And another around Scarlett's apartment. In satellite mode, he scanned the overlapping area, looking for anything out of the ordinary. A block of houses, a petrol station. A building that might have been a school with a small playground. But then Ripper noticed the large grey building on the outskirts of town. It looked like a warehouse.

It didn't take long to find the details. 'Space for Rent,' the webpage said. Ripper called the number and made an appointment.


The information came from the coroner as Ripper was leaving for the warehouse.

"Cause of death seems to be impact to the head." Morten relayed the information in a laconic, exhausted tone. "Judging by the angle, it looks like a fall rather than a blow. Autopsy revealed a build-up of lactic acid in leg muscles. "

It could almost be dismissed as an accident. The victim had been running from something, tripped and hit his head. But that story had a few problems. The position of the body in its surroundings didn't fit. Not unless the man had run straight towards the wall and then tripped, but that made no sense. If he had hit his head on the concrete floor or the brickwork wall, there would've been some detritus in the wound. And if it'd been an accident, why bother to dump the body?

Ripper mulled the information over as the taxi entered an isolated, industrial complex, stopping in front of the warehouse. Ripper rapped his knuckles on the large steel door. A few seconds later, he heard locks grinding, and then the door eased open.

The building manager was affable enough. "Company that hired this thing went bust, so it's just empty space," he explained, showing Ripper into the dusty interior. The lighting was poor but the room was vast. More than big enough for a full-sized track.

"I hire it out mainly for events. Parties and the like."

"Any sports?" Ripper asked. The floor was a little dirty, but a quick sweep would take care of that and he'd skated on worse.

"Nah, we don't have the insurance for those sort of events. Some girls host a rollerdisco once a week though."

Ripper frowned as the caretaker started talking about rates and times. "A rollerdisco?"

"Something like that." The caretaker gave a shrug. "I don't have time to check up on them. I'm not sure of the specifics." Clearing his throat, he gestured to the room. "So, do you reckon you'll be hiring it?"

"I'm not sure yet." Ripper replied. "I'll let you know."

On the way home, questions buzzed through his head. He stopped at the Potomac River, watching the boats go past as he considered the case. It was his favourite part of the city – it had even inspired his derby name – because when he looked out at the water and let his mind drift, even complicated things started to make sense.

Had the building manager misunderstood? Was the warehouse really being hired as a skating rink? Was it even the right venue? There were other sports halls, further out, but his gut told him this was the place. So how did Scarlett and her new league fit into it all?

He was so absorbed in thought that he didn't see the sun setting or the sky turning dark. Not until his phone rang. He fished it from his coat pocket and frowned at the caller ID.

Morten's voice was tight. "We've got an ID on the victim and we've found his car."

"Any leads?" Ripper asked, already heading to a main road to hail a cab.

"We need you to come in and take a look."

"Alright. I'll see you soon."

There had been something odd in the way Morten spoke. As Ripper made his way to the station, he tried to work out what had been hidden in the detective's tone. At the station, he was led to an underground compound, to where a car stood with its trunk open. Looking at the stacks and stacks of skate wheels inside, Ripper realised what he hadn't been able to identify in Morten's tone. Suspicion.

Ripper had known it could get messy when he took the case. As he sat in one of the interrogation rooms, watching Morten set up the recorder, he wondered if it'd been a mistake. Everyone at the station knew he was a referee. But he hadn't seriously expected it to ever be used against him.

"You understand you're not currently being considered a suspect?" Morten queried, settling back into his chair and facing Ripper. "This is entirely voluntary on your part?"

"It is," Ripper said, not liking the emphasis on 'currently'. He'd seen the way the people handling the case were now looking at him. And he figured the simplest way to see what their suspicions were would be to let them ask.

Morten reeled off the date, time and other particulars before commencing the interview. "Would you like to say, in your own words, what we found in the trunk of the victim's car?"

"The trunk was full of rollerskate wheels," Ripper said, seeing no reason to tip-toe around the issue. "Packaged up in fours. Stock to sell, I'd guess."

"Can you think of any reason someone might buy the wheels?"

"To skate with?" Ripper suggested. From the way Morten's forehead developed three extra wrinkles, Ripper guessed his humour wasn't appreciated.

"And who would be skating on this type of wheel?" Morten brought up a bagged pack of wheels. They were a dark green colour with purple lettering. "They're certainly not for kids going up and down the sidewalk," Ripper replied.

"I'm not familiar with the brand. They could be for speed skaters. Or maybe used by the cast of Starlight Express." Seeing that the detective's patience was wearing thin, Ripper relented. "They could also be used for playing roller derby."

"Ah, yes. Roller derby." Morten twisted his mouth, as though the words were unpalatable. "That sport you play. Tell me about it." Ripper shrugged. "It's a skating sport. Fairly new."

"We've looked it up," said Morten, reading something from his notebook. "Full contact, is it?"

"Yes." Ripper wondered if it was better or worse that he hadn't mentioned that before.

"Vicious?"

"Not usually, no."

Morten hummed and made a note before facing Ripper again, a serious gleam in his eyes.

"You've seen the injury believed to have caused the victim's death. Could it have happened through this game?"

"The game is strictly governed," Ripper answered, trying to tread carefully. "By rules to prevent this kind of head injury."

"But rules can be broken sometimes. Can't they?"

"It's possible," Ripper conceded. "But, I've never seen any player-on-player contact that could have caused such a severe injury. The only way something like that could happen was if he collided with the floor or a wall. That could have happened in any kind of skating environment. It could easily have been skateboarding."

"It seems more likely that he was selling those things than using them himself," Morten pointed out. "The injury could have occurred outside of an actual game."

"Or roller derby could be nothing to do with it," Ripper retorted.

Morten fixed Ripper with a penetrating glare. Then spent more time grilling him on the likelihood of derby being involved and any information he had on the wheels. It was another forty minutes before he could leave. Ripper felt himself being watched as he walked out of the station.

Thoughts ricocheted through his mind, but nothing cohesive formed. He could feel the clues milling around in his head. The crucial information was there, he was sure. He just needed to put it together.

He swung by his apartment to pick up his kit, then headed over to the Sportsplex. A good skate always made things clear. There wasn't a scheduled practice, but ever since he'd solved the mystery of who kept flooding the men's showers, he'd been friendly with the staff. They didn't mind him skating when the hall wasn't in use.

Even lacing up his skates was therapeutic. By the time he'd completed a few laps, Ripper was feeling better. He was about to start working on landing a 360 degree jump with a bit more grace, but decided not to. If he fell and got injured, there would be no first-aid. And his impromptu skate sessions weren't insured.

His wheels screeched against the floor as he pulled into a sharp hockey stop. His thoughts slammed to a halt as several things became clear.

He needed to see Scarlett.

Ripper left the cab at a run, not waiting for his change, and took the stairs to Scarlett's apartment two at a time. He hit the landing and slammed straight into her. A pinching around her eyes was the only indication that she was surprised to see him. She hurried past while he was still catching his breath, going down the stairs that he'd just climbed.

"Scarlett -" He caught her at the bottom of the stairs, as she was about to step through the door. "Wait."

She turned without warning, expression hard. There were deep bags under her eyes, faded purple against her skin. "What is it?" As she spoke, she shifted the stuffed duffel bag she carried higher on her shoulder, drawing his attention.

"You're leaving?" Ripper demanded. "But why-"

"You already know the answer to that," said Scarlett with a ghost of a smile. "I'm sure you've figured it out by now."

"But... you didn't. Did you?" Ripper didn't want to believe it.

"It was almost his own fault," Scarlett said, and his heart calmed. "He was a liar and a creep. Selling us faulty gear and denying it when we confronted him. He said he skated on the same equipment, but as you probably realised, that didn't mean much."

"So it was an accident."

"Yes. But we weren't insured. The league wasn't even official, and we were all liable." Scarlett sighed, dragging a hand through her hair. "His death wasn't the crime, it was trying to cover it up. And we thought we could get away with it." She gave him a wry smile. "But here you are."

"You didn't need to hide this," Ripper said, frustrated. "If you'd told me, I could have-"

"Could have what, Ripper?" Scarlett looked at him beseechingly. "You're a referee. You uphold the rules. I wouldn't ask you to jeopardise that. Not for me." A self-deprecating smile. "I knew as soon as you came to see me that you'd taken the case. And that it wouldn't take long before you worked it out."

As she finished talking, a dusty blue car pulled up a few yards away, and Scarlett jerked her thumb towards it. "That's my ride. I've removed all traces that our league ever even existed, but if you tell the cops what you know, it could still come back on us. It's best we're not here if that happens." She gave him a humourless smile.

"Where are you going?" Ripper asked, questions stumbling over one another, out of his mouth. "Will you be back?"

"Europe, maybe. It's not all bad, I've sub-let the apartment so I'll be okay for money, and after the last few months I could do with a break." She shrugged. "Besides, Rollercon's going to be in Berlin this year."

The car driver beeped the horn; Scarlett glanced at it before turning back to face him.

"I have to go." She gave him one last look, lips parting as though to speak, but then turned and walked to the truck without saying another word. She threw her bag in the back, climbed into the passengers' seat and closed the door.

He watched her drive away in silence.


"It's been three months." Morten's frustration was audible. On the other end of the phone, Ripper could picture the expression of consternation the detective would be wearing. "If we don't get a lead in the next few days, we're closing the case. You couldn't turn up anything at all?"

"Sorry." Ripper kept his tone light, not bothering to force false-repentance. "I guess we were unlucky this time."

Morten grumbled for a few minutes more, but eventually hung up. Ripper put his phone away and went back to lacing up his skates.

"Ripper? You still in here?" Vanessa Vanquish – now third-time NSO – stood in the doorway, a clipboard in her hand. "You'll have to come now if we're going to manage the referee meeting before the first whistle."

Ripper followed her to the track. As soon as they left the quiet of the changing room, the noise of the crowd hit them. The excitement was infectious, and even after everything that he'd been through in the last few months, Ripper still smiled as he watched the warming up skaters wave to their fans.

"Before the meeting starts, I wanted to ask you a favour. One of the refs has dropped out for next month and you'd be perfect to fill their place. Ticket and accommodation are already paid for and I'd feel so much more confident knowing you were there."

"Ticket?"

"It's in Berlin. They're holding the first European Rollercon. So what do you say? It'll be a blast: five days of skating and some amazing people."

"When you put it like that," said Ripper, "how can I resist?"

## Elena Morris

*So, that self-defence class turned out to be pretty useless,* I think as I watch a strange man run off with my bag. I should have listened to my instincts telling me that this shortcut to the bus stop was a bad idea. My keys were even in between my fingers as a last resort. Earlier, Mum told me to be careful as she bundled me off the wintry platform and onto my train. I told her not to worry; I could look after myself.

But lying curled up in a ball at the side of the road isn't looking after myself. I'd started crying at the first slap round the face. When I hung onto my bag, begging him not to take it, he'd kneed me in the stomach and ran, swinging my bag behind him. I scrabble in my pockets. *Of course* he took my bus pass and my phone. I'm thankful I have my keys, but I'm four miles away from home.

I almost don't notice the car pulling up beside me on the empty road. I'm torn between hiding behind a parked car and getting up and running, but I hesitate for too long and before I know it there are a pair of combat boots stomping towards me and I'm frozen in a weird half-up, half-down position.

"Are you okay?" asks the owner of the combat boots. "I saw that guy running and... Was that your bag he grabbed off you? Do you know him?"

I stand up and brush myself off, hoping my mascara hasn't run too far down my cheeks. Her heavily pierced face is friendly and her smile is kind and I so badly want to be saved from this situation, but I'm still cautious.

"I don't know him," I say. "He just… he took it."

"And gave you a bit of a beating at the same time?" she asks. I nod. "Look, it's nothing to be ashamed about. I'm Faye, and Molly's in the car. We'll get you home. Where do you live?"

"Up near the library?"

"We'll get you there."

I'm not emotionally equipped to deal with this situation, so the way she takes control makes me trust her. It's not like I have anything else she could take. So I find myself standing outside the car, trying to talk myself into getting in.

"This is Molly," Faye says, gesturing to the driver of the car. She smiles nervously at me, pulling at her long ponytail.

"I'm Rory," I offer. She looks about as freaked out as I feel and I understand why she wouldn't be entirely comfortable with the idea of picking up a stranger in her car and giving her a lift home. It's then that I realise that going home to rattle around my cold, single-glazed studio flat feels like the last thing I want to do right now.

"We're going to be late, Faye," Molly murmurs. "It's the last practice before the bout, if we're not there on time you know there'll be trouble."

Faye's face clouds. I don't know what to do, so I keep quiet.

"You need to call the police anyway, right?" Faye asks me.

"Yeah, and my mum. But I've got no landline, and—"

"Right. How about this? We're going in completely the opposite direction right now but we'll be going your way later. We'll be skating for a couple of hours then heading back, but there's a cafe so I'll lend you some money for something to eat. You can use my mobile while we're skating, then we'll give you a lift back. It'll mean hanging about for a couple of hours, but if you want to then you're welcome to come with us."

It sounds too good to be true. Not only do I get food and access to a phone, I get to stay surrounded by people, instead of replaying what happened over and over, all by myself at home.

I'm still in shock. I can't decide what to do, but Faye must be able to tell I'm wavering.

"We'll stick to main roads, and we're going to a sports centre with security. You'll be safe."

The word safe does it. The same gut feeling that told me not to take the short-cut to the bus stop is now telling me to trust them. I get in the car.

Turns out, my instincts were right again. The skating they're talking about is roller derby, a sport that feels like it's been on the tip of my tongue for a long time. That first practice, I get a sandwich with the handful of spare coins Molly finds in her glove compartment, then use Faye's phone to call the police. They take the details, but soon fob me off saying that there's not much they can do. After that I phone my Mum who offers to drive a 400-mile round trip so she can look after me, but I reassure her it's not necessary while trying to find my way back to the hall.

As I walk back in, I'm confronted with the sight of about twenty women on skates beating the ever-living crap out of each other. They're fully padded up and they're hitting each other with their shoulders, hips, bums, chests, and when they fall they get straight back up. No one takes any notice of me stood in the doorway with my mouth getting wider and wider until I hang up the phone and hear myself asking if I can have a go.

I feel like I was born to be on eight wheels. I fly around the outside of the track in my borrowed skates and pads and I learn how to do knee falls and t-stops. My lost bag is pushed from my mind. I'm getting another shot of adrenaline, but this time it's different. The energy coursing through my body isn't from fear; it's from exhilaration. I promise to attend the bout next week and then their fresh meat intake the week after.

Three weeks down the line and I'm spending £150 of my phone insurance money on a 'derby starter kit' with skates, pads, helmet and mouthguard. Falling still hurts, and I'm doing it a lot – sometimes deliberately, but not always. When I crash out at home in the evenings, I'm looking up bout footage online instead of watching TV, because I want to understand *everything* about derby. I print out the rules and bury myself in them during lunch breaks. I skate around car parks and quiet roads with Faye and Molly twice a week, and I can feel myself getting quietly stronger.

The first few practices, I come home sweating, horrified at how sweaty my knees can get. After the next few, I throw up from over-exertion. I'm trying as hard as I can, but I'm still not as good as the others. It stings when I catch a smirk in my direction as I fluff up a baseball slide. Then I start throwing up before practice as well from nerves. Nerves that I'm not good enough or that I'm not pushing myself hard enough or that I'm going to get kicked out.

At practice number ten, Faye is off sick and I feel the lack of her encouragement. I'm worn out, and afterwards I burst into tears in the passenger seat of Molly's car. She pats me awkwardly on the shoulder. I decide to quit.

I have to go back just once because I don't want to email the coaches; I want to tell them face-to-face that I'm leaving. I find myself lacing up my skates and participating in the usual gruelling warm-up. *Just five more minutes,* I'm saying to myself. *Five more minutes until I tell them.* But then before I know it, I'm standing on the jammer line with the stars on my helmet.

I get up onto my toe-stops but lose my balance, and it's a good three seconds after the starting whistle before I've even set off. I can hear laughs from my fellow skaters – some kind, some mean – and my face floods red. I squash down the part of my brain that tells me I'm not good enough, and slowly skate from side to side, trying to find a path through the wall of women in front of me. I try to hop about, falling in the process, but I carry on bluffing and double bluffing until there it is – a gap. I leap through and start skating my diamond around the track. The whoops and cheers fly through me like electricity. I feel like I might cry because all the bruises and the sweat and the vomit are now a clear part of my path. It lights up before me and I can see myself, for the first time, as an athlete.

I start treating my body with more respect and I'm aware of the muscles in my thighs becoming more and more defined. The day I flex my bicep in the mirror for the first time is the day I join a gym. All the money I saved on moving to a dangerous area of the city by myself, a hundred miles away from home and anyone I've ever known, it all goes on roller derby. I'm like an animal; I can't be stopped. I'm fresh meat, then a rookie, then B-team. Nine months fly past and I'm running every single morning to increase my endurance and make my way up to the A-team.

When I skate, I feel powerful. I feel the wheels of my skates hit the floor and I feel my calves and shins take that impact and transfer it up to my thighs. I feel my strong arms pumping at my sides. I feel something that two years of working as a general dogsbody on TV sets could never make me feel: I matter. I am important. I am training so that my teammates can depend on me to give them a whip when they need it, and so I can put on that extra burst of speed to get me through a miniscule gap and score that winning point. I am Roary. Hear me roar.

The violence is structured. I am hit, and I hit back. I spend hours working on my core strength and my oblique muscles, until I can simultaneously twist my top half around and push my shoulder into someone's sternum while skating. I become a deadly weapon in the A-team's arsenal, and I soak in the sense of achievement for days.

But all the time, in the back of my head, I've been thinking about karma. That man took my bag but he gave me roller derby. He took something, but he gave me something too, and I can't quite figure out where that lies on the karmic scale. I don't know if he still owes me anything, but the punch bag at my gym is certain he does, as are the heavy doors at work and every single girl I hit on my journey to the A-team.

The first frost of the year comes on the evening I break Molly's rib with my shoulder. She wears her usual stony-faced mask but I can tell that it's agony for her. It takes a long time for Faye to manoeuvre Molly's car along the icy roads to A&E, and Molly winces with every jolt. I warm her hand with both of mine and hold a paper bag to her mouth when she throws up from the pain. The next day, I am drained after seven hours in A&E followed by a ten-hour shift at work, but I have something that buoys me. Something that puts a bounce in my step, even in my 36th straight hour of staying awake. I have a sisterhood.

So maybe I let my guard down. I've been taking the dodgy shortcut home for weeks now, but this time I keep my earbuds in because I feel strong and safe and that means I can listen to music even while walking through unsafe neighbourhoods. I shift my heavy skate bag onto my shoulder more securely but as I pull, there is resistance. The hand grabbing my shoulder takes me by surprise, as does the fist in my jaw. When I refuse to relinquish my bag, the knee in my stomach hurts just as much as it did before I had washboard abs. *But wait!* I'm thinking, *I didn't have time to engage my core!* He sprints away with my smelly kit bag, my purse and my phone and I'm left doubled over in pain on the pavement again. All I can really think is, *wait until he gets a whiff of my wristguards.* And then, *I needed new skates anyway.*

**Kat M. Gray**

The Conch Republic was nothing special for a Key West bar. But it was a strange place for Lucie York, member of the Key West Ballet Theatre, to find herself on a Wednesday.

"Key West is a circus," her dance instructor José Callero said, when he was welcoming the new troupe of dancers. "You are part of that illusion, but do not become consumed by it."

That meant no bars. Until now, Lucie had behaved.

Girls of every description ringed tables of mismatched patio furniture. One girl had a bright pink and black mohawk, and her friend's chest was covered in parrot-bright tattoos. Another had hair pulled back into a plain ponytail and was dressed in a racerback tee and workout capris. Lucie felt a twinge of jealousy at such unapologetic strength; her own muscles almost seemed demure comparatively. A ballet dancer had to have pleasing lines, not bulging biceps.

Lucie stuck out like the toe she'd banged against the door a few months ago. She had to dance on it anyway, but she grimaced every time she went up on point, and Callero hadn't let her forget a single facial tic.

The lithe dancer picked her way through the crowd to a table in the corner. Too late, she saw information packets at the centre table.

The girl handing them out had wild black ringlets cascading down her back.

Lucie could spot her bright blue eyes from the corner, and a nose piercing gleamed in her skin. Key West Rollin' Rogues was scrawled across her t-shirt in metallic reds and purples, and below that was a girl in full roller derby gear. A pirate bandanna pinned back her wild hair and she clenched a cutlass in her teeth; her wristguarded hands clutched a rope, and she swung forward kicking one skate up at the viewer's face.

That was when Lucie realised that the ringleted girl was staring back. Lucie flushed crimson and dug for her notebook in her bag, but not before she'd seen the girl smirk right at her.

"You've had enough beer to get your courage up," she called. Lucie could tell it was her without looking. "So why don't we kick this thing off? I'm Murderous Molly Mutiny, or M3, and I'm captain of the Rollin' Rogues. We're the only flat track team in the Keys, and we've been around for about seven months. I assume most of you gals are here because you know a little bit about derby and you want to go for it." She stopped, and caught Lucie's eye. "But just in case, I'll show you a video of what we do."

M3 aimed a remote at the wall-mounted TV.

PSYCHO CITY SICKOS GREATEST HITS!

The neon yellow headline faded into an amateur video of a team dressed in the same yellow, paired with silver and black, skating against a team in turquoise and white. Lucie's head swam trying to keep up with the faster skaters' flashy footwork and the large group of girls on the track mixing around one another like they were in a clothes dryer.

BAM! A girl in neon suddenly swooped across the track and nailed a girl in turquoise who wore a helmet with a star. The girl went airborne, fell to the ground on her knees and elbows, then rolled once... twice! To Lucie's surprise, the girl with the star was soon scrambling back upright, chasing down her assailant for another try.

Lucie didn't even feel her neck cramp until the end credits (set to Alice Cooper's Welcome to My Nightmare) started to roll. She searched for M3 in the crowd and found her standing front and centre, a Cheshire cat grin taking up most of her face.

"That's what we do – skate fast, hit hard. So I'm gonna turn this over to our head of training, Tessa Tortuga, and let her talk to you about the details."

Tessa was slim like Lucie, but every muscle was finely drawn. She wasn't much taller than M3, but her frame was more willowy. Lucie wondered how she could take massive hits like the one in the video. But as soon as Tessa opened her mouth, her voice was not soft and musical, but tough and playful, as though she dared anyone to interrupt her and live to tell the tale.

The questions from the audience were swift. How long before you could play? What kind of skates were best? Where did the team travel?

Lucie had no questions that she wanted to ask aloud. How bad were the injuries? How often did they happen? What would this sport do to her feet, already perfectly callused for dancing?

An hour passed before attention returned to M3. She was all smiles, like a shark.

M3 crossed her arms over her chest. "It seems like a lot to take in all at once, but I can promise you, all it takes is one time skating with a team. This sport is not right for everybody, but if it's your thing, the sport will let you know. I've been doing this a while – and I can tell you which girls in this room will stick with derby, and which ones will give it up."

Her eyes went straight to Lucie, then casually flitted away. Lucie looked around the room and noticed Mohawk and Tattoos whispering as they looked away.

"We gotta get out of here before they kick us out," M3 continued, "but take your packets with you. They've got waivers inside, and we need you to sign those if you're going to skate with us. Remember, practice two nights from now, at the Rogues' Gallery, corner of Seminary and Grinnell. We'll have skates and pads for you if you need to rent 'em, but if you're serious about this, you need to start saving up for your own gear as soon as possible. Now let's get outta here before we get 'asked to leave'."

Her fingers hitched sarcastic air quotes to the phrase, and wooden chairs scraped over the floor. Lucie shoved her notebook into her messenger bag, her face hot. She wondered if M3 had meant to single her out. She couldn't decide which was worse – getting singled out here or getting picked apart by one of Callero's notorious rants.

She was halfway to the door before she realised she didn't have an info packet. She darted back to a table and snatched one up, not realising it was soaked in beer until she it was in her hand. Oh well – she could dry it. With M3's words ringing in her ears, she ducked out the door and into the August night.


Lucie's roommate Aisling came home from rehearsal to find Lucie drying papers in the bathroom. She breezed past, but then Lucie heard her backtrack. Tall, mocha-skinned, sculpted to a ballerina's elegant proportions like she was cut out from a catalogue, Aisling raised one eyebrow at her roommate.

"What the hell are you doing?" After a four-hour practice for the ballet opening in a few weeks' time, Aisling didn't even *sound* exhausted.

Lucie flicked off the hairdryer and set it down, shutting the folder to show the front cover with the Rollin' Rogues' logo.

"Drying off my info packet. It got covered in beer."

"Info packet -" Aisling started to say. She looked down at the cover. "Oh shit. You actually *went* to that meeting?"

Lucie shrugged. "I said I was going to."

Aisling leant against the doorway. "I figured you were just joking after that night Callero busted your balls."

Lucie liked Aisling. But she was so serious about her career as a dancer. Aisling was KWBT's finest solo ballerina, and Lucie couldn't help being jealous. Feeling plain, as she always did when she was near Aisling, Lucie ran her fingers through her hair, still wavy from the tight braid she usually wore to class, even though she'd taken it out hours ago.

"Aisling, I need a break from getting chewed out."

Callero was hard on all of his students, but Lucie felt he was much harder on her than the others. Aisling, though, came from Florida State's School of Dance, and told hair-rising stories about the way the teachers there had talked to the students.

"The only reason Callero talks to you that way is because he wants you as his lead *pas des deux* dancer. Not Fancy Nancy."

Nancy Deville had not yet discovered that choreographers did not like alternative interpretations.

"He wants me as his lead dancer so much he puts me down every chance he gets."

"He's just trying to make you better," Aisling said. That was always her point of view. "You need to lighten up."

"That's what I'm *trying* to do," Lucie said, waving the Rollin' Rogues packet at her. Aisling made a face as stale, cheap beer wafted her way.

"Whatever you say," Aisling said, detaching herself from her post at the door frame. "But you know if Callero finds out, he'll chew your ass into hamburger meat."

The Rogues' Gallery was a warehouse, not a skating rink. The floor was dark pitted concrete with a rough chalk circle track. There were a handful of taped lines.

The skates Lucie rented didn't fit quite right. The toes pinched her already aching feet, and the rest of the black leather boot looked awfully banged up. She made out the word "Riedell" on the velcro strap over the tatty laces, but it meant nothing to her.

Several of the girls from the meeting had showed up. Tessa strapped and taped them into hand-me-down gear, gathered them into a semi-circle, and announced that she'd be leading fresh meat practice.

*Fresh meat,* Lucie thought, frowning.

It was pretty much what she felt like, though. And it was no different than the way she'd felt when she'd walked into her first rehearsal with the theatre.

Tessa was brief. They'd be learning basic skating skills. A good stance, how to take strong strides, how to stop, and the proper way to fall.

There was a proper way? The last time Lucie had actually skated was a birthday party for her best friend when they were seven. She remembered flailing spindly little arms and legs all over the place, and wiping out on the cool wood floor like she was being given style points. It hadn't even hurt.

This skating *did* hurt, though. Lucie's back and legs started to ache while learning what Tessa called crossovers. For speed, she said. Lucie was starting to get them, and finally her skates weren't making clomping sounds.

"Faster!" shouted Tessa. Lucie pushed harder.

She could feel her own speed now, and the way that her body naturally leaned into a turn when she did her crossovers like Tessa said. She bit down on her lip, repeating the instructions to herself like a mantra. *Push, cross, push...*

She went over a spot in the floor that looked shiny just as she pushed, hard, with her inside foot. The world went a little sideways then, and she reached out with her hands to stop it from spinning. She didn't know that her borrowed knee-pad had slipped down until the side of her knee bottomed out painfully against the hard floor. So much for duct tape fixing everything. Lucie cried out and looked down at her knee more in panic than in pain. Was it swelling?

"Three second recovery time! You'll never catch the pack if you just lie there after you fall!" M3 called, sailing by with the advanced skaters.

Tessa grabbed Lucie by her forearms and stood her back up.

"Whoops, looks like you had a little slip," Tessa said, leaning down and taping Lucie's kneepad tighter around her slender leg. "You alright? Good to go on?"

Lucie nodded, ignoring the throbbing in her kneecap. No way in hell would she sit out.


The next morning, Lucie's right kneecap looked like a purple, swollen tangerine. It showed through her flesh-coloured tights, but there was no helping it. She had tried covering it with powder and concealer. She had tried wearing two pairs of tights. The last thing she wanted was somebody asking where that bruise came from, and she *had* to go to *pas des deux* class today to learn their next audition piece.

Lucie found herself caught up in memorising the steps, working on coordinating her movements with her partner, Felix Vincenza. He was dark-skinned, dark-eyed, very Cuban, very handsome, and very gay. Aisling was always complaining to him about that part. He always answered by asking her what she expected from a male ballerina in Key West.

Finally, each pair had to demonstrate the choreography. Callero's critiques were fierce. Most pairs didn't make it to the initial lift because he'd stop them before they ever got there, picking at simple things like turnout, or the strain on a male dancer's face as his hand almost slipped while lifting his partner.

Lucie closed her eyes for a moment as the floor cleared for her and Felix. The music began, and it lifted her, lightening her body so that she was tiptoeing on clouds. The initial sequence was discordant – two lovers fighting to clasp hands across a raging river. It meant fast feet, sharp angles of the legs and arms. The precision required for it was unforgiving; one of the other dancers had even stumbled over her own feet trying to get it right.

Lucie floated through the initial sequence, her feet light and almost soundless on the floor. Then she reached for Felix's hand, felt his tentative hope – *finally, the storm has ceased...*

"Stop!"

Lucie froze, just as she'd been expecting that feeling of flight from Felix's lift. The magic had been deflated, but you could only see it in her eyes – they were back front and centre as she folded her hands at her waist and waited to hear what she'd done wrong.

"Beautiful lines and angles, Miss York, and the emotion on your face was exquisite. Longing, but brave, daring to cross to reach your beloved. Felix, you showed great precision, though your emotion needs to be *felt* much more deeply. The lift, I'm sure, would have been exquisite. But..."

Lucie frowned. "But?" This was practically the highest praise she'd ever received from the hard-nosed Spaniard.

"What is *that*?" Callero said, pointing quite clearly at Lucie's knee.

Lucie looked down. Under the hard white studio lights, the bruise looked worse; a sullen, ugly bluish bulge.

"A bruise," Lucie answered. "I... I was walking back home from work and I tripped over an uneven spot in the sidewalk."

"You tripped?" Callero said, raising his dark eyebrows. "Maybe you should show as much grace when you walk as you did just now, eh?"

Callero's accent became thicker when he made remarks such as these. There were several barely suppressed titters among her classmates. He turned to them suddenly.

"Laugh all you want, but if an apparently clumsy ballerina can dance the *pas des deux* with that much technical skill, what is the excuse for the rest of you?"

Lucie's face burned. She caught Aisling's eyes in the mirror. Her look was pointed, and easily readable.

*I told you so.*

It had been almost two months now, and Lucie was still skating, despite Aisling telling her stupid she was on an almost hourly basis. In between derby and dance, she barely had any energy to go work her waitress job at Nine on the Line, a sports-themed bar and grill.

In the meantime, Tessa Tortuga had taught Lucie how to use foundation to cover up the bruises after Lucie had told her about the trouble in class. Tessa had learned from Piranha, a make-up artist on the team. Add that to the list of random careers Lucie had learned her teammates had.

Sasha Kalashnikov, Tessa's derby wife, was a locksmith. Sasha made Lucie a key to the Rogues' Gallery so she could skate more often. Lucie's rehearsals, especially as they neared opening night for *Coppelia,* were taking up a lot of the extra evenings she would have had to fine-tune her basic skills at the warehouse. It was driving her insane; Lucie didn't do anything without trying to do it well. So, she had asked Tessa what to do, and this had been Tessa's solution.

"You can't tell a soul," Tessa said, when she handed over the key, her gray-blue eyes serious. "Especially not M3. If she finds out, I'm toast, and I don't even *know* what she'll do to you."

That hadn't stopped Lucie from taking the key.

Mondays and Wednesdays were solo classes, then work, then skating. Tuesdays and Thursdays, early morning endurance skates – 100 laps. It took her forever at first. Lucie hadn't missed a single league practice, either; Thursday nights and Sunday mornings like clockwork, she was there.

"You're more devoted to *that* than you are to the company," Aisling had remarked recently.

Lucie had thought for a moment about it, but there really wasn't any use in arguing – Aisling was right.

"Dance is an art, dance is a *gift,*" Aisling had argued, impassioned.

In its own way, roller derby was brutal poetry, Lucie thought, but she couldn't have explained that to her roommate. Lucie sweated at dance rehearsals, but it wasn't the same as the way she did at Rogues' practice. As she swiped the sweat off her face with a washcloth in the shower after skating, her body still ached, but she wouldn't have thought even once to complain about it. This was pain that reminded her of fearlessness and grit, not the cool sacrifice of precision and the implacable lines of her face during a performance – no anger, no pain, but no joy either.

The Wednesday evening before her skills assessment, Lucie unlocked the deadbolt to let herself in. Her stomach flipped as she sat down to gear up. For whatever reason, Lucie always found dress rehearsal more nerve-wracking than the actual performance. She had the sheet of required skills, and she was just going to run through them once and call it a night. If she was satisfied, at least, though that wasn't likely. But inside, she heard voices carrying from the office. Between the two of them, she soon recognised Tessa.

"It's not like all of those girls dropped off the face of the earth, Molly. Some people just don't have what it takes for this. We're lucky to get five strong skaters out of any recruitment drive."

Molly. Dear God. Lucie hoped they stayed wherever they were instead of coming in to the track.

"There's got to be something we're doing wrong." M3 was insistent. "We've only kept three of them full-time, and another four or five that show up whenever the fuck they feel like it."

"Maybe Key West is not a derby town like we thought it was," Tessa responded. "I mean, it's going to take some time to get this rolling. We haven't even been around a year yet."

"Not yet, but it's damn close enough that people should know who we are!" M3 snapped. "Key West is *crawling* with women who would eat this up, and I can't figure out why they're not beating down our doors. There has to be something we're doing wrong – promotion, training... I don't know."

Silence. Finally, Tessa spoke.

"Look, can we just talk about the fresh meat evaluations I have planned? I'm gonna need some track time next Thursday."

"Evaluations?!" M3 exploded. "They can hardly hold on to a corner when they sprint!"

"Look," Tessa said, "I know some of them still have work to do, but the three that are coming regularly are ready to test. Morgan only needs to work on her stops and her crossovers, and she'll be fine."

"Yeah, because those things are easily learned in a week," M3 said sourly.

"Well, Bridget and Lucie are definitely ready."

Silence again. Lucie squeezed her eyes shut.

"Bridget. She falls if you blow on her."

"Stability can be worked on, you know that. I've been giving her core exercises."

"Too bad they're not helping. And don't even get me started on Tiptoes."

"Lucie's put in a lot of work to get where she is," Tessa said, intervening before Molly could, in fact, get started on 'Tiptoes'.

"Yeah, she comes to practice. What about it?"

"Lucie skates five days a week. You can't deny her fitness level. Her skating technique... she just needs to get a little lower. Everything else, she's been working on."

"What, in her sleep? That dance schedule she gave me for whatever thing it is they're putting on in a month or so is *ridiculous.* Do you think she can make the commitment?" M3 said.

"I *know* she can, Molly. You have no idea how much time she puts in outside of her classes and work, and I can verify that for you, right down to the hour."

Silence again. This time, it was M3 who broke it.

"Tessa..."

"What?" Tessa sounded defensive. Lucie started stuffing gear back into her bag.

"Did you give her a key? Did you give her a fucking key to *our warehouse* before she's even passed her assessment?"

"Yes, okay? And I don't care if that's against our by-laws," Tessa answered. "She wanted to know where she could get skate time in, and dammit, Molly, this is the best choice for miles around. I've never found a single piece of equipment out of place after she's visited... and we've never had a fresh meat who *tried* so hard. You said it yourself, we don't have people beating down our doors. We *need* skaters like Lucie."

"So she can put in hours of practice. She's a little frou-frou ballerina, she's used to that. But there's something you're missing."

"What's that?"

"She doesn't have the *guts,* Tessa, she just doesn't. The second she gets out there to bout, the other team will smell it on her like blood in the water. Hell, I'm not sure our own team won't tear her to pieces when she starts scrimmaging. The first time she gets knocked out of her skates by Sasha she'll go running back home. Ballet and derby *don't* mix."

Lucie felt the muscles in her gut clench roughly, knotting around Molly's statement like an oyster around a grain of sand. She didn't tear up, but sometimes, after Callero had lit her on fire, she wouldn't cry until she got home. Right now, she just wanted to go home. The hell with practising. She needed to think this over.

Lucie yanked the warehouse key off of her keyring, snatched a piece of paper from her notebook and scribbled 'sorry' on it. Tessa's purse was hanging on a peg near the door. Lucie dropped both the key and the note inside.

She was quiet as she left, taking almost ten full seconds to close the door – it squealed like a piglet on the way shut, something she'd learned from being here so often over the past few weeks. Tension had started to crawl up the muscles of her neck now, making both them and her head ache. She forced her feet into motion, but didn't realise how fast she'd been walking until she got home and found herself covered with sweat.

It wasn't until the next morning that she realised she hadn't cried.

On test night, Lucie put on her gear quietly. She imagined the proper form for the knee drops, the precision of the diamond she would skate for her timed laps. She did this before performances – a habit she'd picked up from Aisling. This time, she found that her anger at Molly still simmered, and that kept her centred.

Tessa interrupted.

"Look, Lucie, Molly says stuff she doesn't mean sometimes... I mean, she would never have wanted you to hear that."

"Water under the bridge," said Lucie, through clenched teeth.

Tessa stood there until Lucie looked up. Lucie didn't have to ask whether Tessa believed a single word she'd just said.

Lucie was fastest on the timed laps. Then, it was on to skills. M3 had insisted on rating the skaters. That was just as well for Lucie. Being aware of that particular set of blue eyes on her the entire time sparked something within her. Something even Callero couldn't reach with his critiques, which had continued hot and heavy in the past few weeks. Too tired at practice. Muscles too shaky – was she still cross training? Was she still on the diet?

*Yes, I am.* That was all she said.

Once the test was over, it was a long few minutes as M3 tallied the scores. No worse than waiting to hear after an audition, Lucie told herself. But there was something that leaped and spun inside her throat, more frantic by the second. She didn't know if her body was planning for her to throw up or start yelling in triumph. She had never wanted a role in a ballet this badly. She *had* to pass. The alternative felt like being stuck, her eight wheels spinning in quicksand forever.

"Morgan... you passed everything but your baseball slide," M3 said, addressing the girl with the cropped copper hair who sat to Lucie's left. "You can retake it in a week, but until then, you're still meat."

The girl's face fell, but Lucie didn't crack – not yet anyway. She was next in line, and M3 was about to let her have it. She knew that. But M3 turned her head to Bridget, the blonde pony-tailed girl who was full of attitude and had been 100% derby from day one, dressing to the nines in bright tights, tutus, and cut up t-shirts at every practice. She at least *looked* the part.

"Bridget, your stability is still not where it needs to be, and that's a problem with your skating form. Next time you come to practice, I want a 5k down in speed skating position the entire time. I don't care if it takes you three hours. If you want to move on to the next level you have *got* to get that down."

Lucie wondered if she'd come back.

"And Miss Lucie," M3 said, letting Lucie drown in silence for a moment. "Seems like you've been working hard on those skills, ballerina. You pass."

Lucie couldn't help but smile, energy surging inside her not unlike it did when the spotlights first hit her during a performance.

"You join us in scrimmage practice on Sunday," M3 said, like she was dropping a nuclear bomb. It had its effect. Lucie's smile froze. "Oh, and one more thing... now you get to pick your derby name. What's it gonna be?"

"Tiptoes." The word was out of her mouth, loud and strong-voiced, before she could even think. She'd even had another name in mind.

M3 didn't let it crack her. "Aren't you precious?" she said coolly. "See you Sunday, girls."

It was victory, and Lucie felt it as she stripped off her pads. Tessa met her at the door on the way out.

"Lucie, that was ballsy," she said, raising her eyebrows. "But I hope it wasn't a mistake."

"We'll find out," Lucie said, allowing her lips to curve in a tiny smile. The streets seemed to have a surreal misty glow as she walked home, savouring the aches and pains in her muscles. She deserved that name.


Lucie floated through her technique class Friday morning and had found Callero's ranting in *pas des deux* Friday afternoon amusing.

By Sunday, it was a different story. She was, geared up (finally) in her own pads. The skates were still loaners until her next paycheck, but piece by piece, Tiptoes was becoming a derby girl. Tessa gave her the basics of hitting at the beginning of the practice and then sent her off to drill with the rest of the team.

Her first scrimmage drill. She felt like she should get a certificate for even making it *this* far, but in front of her, there were muscular Amazons and sleek panthers. They were all sharp, precise edges and she was a rusty pocket knife.

M3 called the drill Endless Jammer. Lucie had seen it before, and she wondered how the nimble jammers made it through four girls all by themselves. The odds seemed impossible.

Lucie started in the pack. She didn't know where to look, and missed the first jammer who came through, earning a ferocious glare from M3.

"Watch your damn outside!"

From then on, Lucie did. Even when she couldn't keep up anymore, she still tried a hit or two. The one or two 'nice jobs' she got just for trying were worth their weight in bearings. M3 called a water break. Lucie wasn't picked for the next pack.

"Ladies," M3 said, "we're breaking in a new jammer this round, so please be careful when our lil' Tiptoes comes through... she's only had her first hitting lesson tonight."

M3 whistled them back onto the track. Lucie took the jammer panty that someone offered her and situated it awkwardly on her helmet. Somewhere around the middle of the line, she made her approach to the pack.

"JAMMER UP!"

M3's voice was a lioness roar. Lucie saw shapes moving in front of her, blockers shifting to look over their shoulders. *Move your feet,* she reminded herself. She made Kona Kickass think she was timid, then darted past. In front, there was a three-wall. She measured distance like when she tried to hit her mark on the stage.

Sasha. She hit hard, but moved too slow, and she was on the outside. The pack was fast, and Sasha was hanging back on the right side of the wall. Lucie had only one shot.

She juked to the very outside, then cut back in to shoot in front of the wall. In slow motion, Sasha went for the hit. It raked across Lucie's chest and lifted her up in the air. She was falling backwards, and there was nothing she could do.

"Are you alright? Lucie, answer me."

Tessa's face hovered over her, and she realized that the halo she wore was just the glare from the harsh lights overhead.

That brought her to her own head, which hurt.

"What the hell just happened..."

There was relieved laughter.

"Sasha happened," Tessa said, smiling. "You took a sheriff to the chest and went over backwards. Did you hit your head?"

"I bumped it a little," Lucie lied, "but my butt and my shoulders took most of it."

"Alright, up and over to the bench," Tessa said. Lucie wanted to protest, but Tessa headed it off. "We'll get you some water and let you rest for a second. That's a hard fall to take in your first scrimmage drill."

"Need to work on that derby stance," M3 commented. "Stay low, and hits like those will miss you, or you'll at least be able to take them better than that."

It was bitter medicine to admit M3 was right.


Lucie threw up in the bushes on the way home. It took her a good three tries to get the key in the apartment's deadbolt. As she squinted at it in the dusk of their neon-lit street, the lock seemed to change location...

"Aisling..." Lucie called as she stumbled in. She stood on her toes rummaging through their medicine cabinet and realising how much it hurt to tilt her head backwards. "Do you have your migraine medicine?"

Lucie needed to get this pain to stop so she could sleep, but aspirin wasn't going to do the trick. The *real* trick here would be keeping Aisling from finding out why she had the headache in the first place.

"Yeah, girl," Aisling said, coming from the back room with the little orange bottle. She handed one to Lucie, who immediately filled her cupped hand with water at the sink. She choked down the pill as quickly as possible – now, she could get herself together for technique class in the morning and *pas des deux* in the afternoon.

Aisling watched her, pressing one palm against the counter to support her slim form.

"You okay?"

"You know how I get headaches when I get dehydrated."

"Yeah." Lucie hoped Aisling didn't know concussion symptoms.

"Just gonna go crash," Lucie murmured.

She winced when Aisling sighed.

"Your pupils look dilated and you're weaving like a drunk."

"I'm fine... I've been walking home in the dark, whatcha expect 'em to look like."

Even Lucie could hear the slur in her speech. She tried to make eye contact with Aisling, but her face seemed just slightly out of focus, the proper points to look at just a little obscured.

*I'm just tired...*

"Miss York, I need to see you in Administration," Callero said.

Had her tuition cheque bounced? Lucie was a fastidious about her finances, but it was no lie to say derby was draining her bank balance.

She dressed in a loose set of jazz pants and her dance sneakers, pulling on a KWBT t-shirt over her leotard. Her head was throbbing as though it was about to burst, so she unpinned her bun, which looked much more unruly than usual.

The Administrative Office was painted Pepto Bismol pink, furnished with pink and brown brocade chairs, and was one of the least pleasant places Lucie had ever been. Callero didn't usually come in here either, so this must have been a special occasion.

"Miss York," said Callero precisely. "Would you explain this?"

He turned the computer monitor to face her. There it was: the Key West Rollin' Rogues website. "Tiptoes, #XIV." Along the left side of the page, there was a headshot. It was the same headshot on the Theatre's Dancer Biographies page. Her name, her number, her picture, and the words "Bio Coming Soon!"

"Is there something that should be explained?" she heard herself saying. It didn't sound like her quavering, polite voice.

"Maybe explain why you thought it was a wonderful idea for a member of a professional ballet troupe to join a team of women who beat each other up on skates?"

"It's good cross-training," Lucie said dryly.

"This is unacceptable! I'm not going to have my best *pas des deux* dancer wasting two nights a week! I will not have you performing in my ballets with bruises all over your body, and I will not have you ruin your feet with roller-skating!"

Lucie bit her tongue. Yelling wouldn't help.

"You have choices, Miss York. Either roller derby goes, or Key West Ballet Theatre goes. It's up to you."

"Really?" Lucie said. She couldn't help but sound sarcastic. "You're going to tell me what I can do with my free time?"

Callero burst.

"When your free time involves getting concussions, yes! When you are participating in a dangerous contact sport that could end a possibly brilliant career early, yes! How could you be so irresponsible with your body?"

"I understand," Lucie said, feeling her resistance drain out of her.

She stood to leave, letting Callero think that she'd made the right choice. The truth was, she hadn't made any choice – not yet.

Well, except for one. There was only *one* way Callero could have found out about her concussion.

Lucie was packed before Aisling came home from work the next day. She could only put so much in Tessa's car, and Tessa would be here within the hour.

Aisling stopped by Lucie's bedroom, as usual. This time, a raised eyebrow wasn't even an option.

"Lucie, what the hell are you doing?"

"What does it look like?" Lucie's voice wasn't sarcastic. It was hard, though, like something inside her had crystallised, like the oyster formed out of M3's critiques had finally produced not a pearl, but a glittering, rough diamond. A stone that could cut all other stones.

Put-together Aisling couldn't find the words. When she spoke, it was ten long seconds later, and in a softer voice.

"You can't just move out of here. What gives? Is something wrong back home?"

"Nope."

"You're on the contract until June, you know."

"Find a sub-leaser."

Aisling grabbed Lucie's hand before she could pack the t-shirt she was holding.

"We're friends... you're just going to leave without even telling me?"

Lucie pulled her arm free from Aisling's and packed her t-shirt. For the first time that Aisling could remember, Lucie looked unforgiving.

"We're friends? What right does a friend have to tell Callero what I'm doing in my free time to try to stop me doing it? What kind of friend is that, Aisling?"

"Lucie, that's not fair."

"No shit it's not fair! You took something important to me and almost lost me my job."

"Not fair?" Aisling suddenly lost her composure. "You're blowing it, Luce. All this talent. Callero wants to make you a star, and you could go *anywhere* after this... is skating that important?"

"I don't know. And I don't have to answer to you, *or* your ideas about what I need to do with my life."

Lucie stuffed another handful into her suitcase. Aisling watched. There was a horn outside and Lucie zipped the bag shut with a ferocity she'd never known herself to have.

"That's my ride," she said. "I'll be back over the next few days to get the rest."

There was no goodbye, messy or otherwise.

Lucie's bags barely fit into Tessa's little Miata.

"You sure about this?" Tessa asked as Lucie buckled her seatbelt. Lucie smiled at her wearily.

"No. Not yet, anyway."

Tessa said, "I've got you a place to stay... but you may hate me for it."


M3 did not seem surprised when she found Tessa and an overburdened Lucie on her porch.

"Welcome to mi casa," she said. Tessa took Lucie's bags to the guest room in the back of the small tangerine-coloured one-storey.

"I've got work in the morning," Tessa said as she came back up the hallway. "You two should get settled. Lucie's had a shitty couple of days."

Tessa and M3 talked like old friends, with a familiarity that Lucie envied – she'd never had friends that close at KWBT. Not even Aisling. Especially not Aisling.

M3 locked the door, then turned to Lucie. "Want a glass of water?"

Lucie nodded. M3 brought it to her, complete with a coaster shaped like a seashell. Lucie drank. She couldn't help but smile as she set the glass back down.

"What's that for?" M3 asked.

"M3 just doesn't seem like the type of girl to use kitschy fifties seashell coasters."

M3 smiled. It was mystifying, because it seemed to have no hidden meaning. "Call me Molly."

"I won't stay long, I promise," Lucie said. "Just until I can find something temporary."

"Uh-uh," Molly said, shaking her head. Lucie noticed the neat pincurls holding back her bangs, and her sleek ponytail, pinned back with rhinestone barrettes. "This *is* your something temporary. I'm not looking for a roommate, but I'm not going to let you move into some flophouse just because you think you're an inconvenience. I've got a shed out back where you can put anything that won't fit in the guest room."

"Thanks," Lucie said. Her throat was dry. Her eyes flicked up to Molly, then down to the coffee table.

"Derby girls are full of surprises, Tiptoes," Molly said. This time, her smile was secretive. She held her words for a moment, then looked steadily at her teammate. "I owe you an apology."

Lucie was quiet. A week ago, she would have agreed.

"I don't take it personally... anymore," Lucie said, smiling. "Besides, you were right."

Molly tilted her head curiously. "About what?"

"Ballet and derby *don't* mix."


It took a week of missing classes for Lucie to find the right words. She skated 200 laps at the Rogues' Gallery the morning she took the envelope to the KWBT mailbox.

When Callero opened his mail, he found a handwritten letter. The stationery was powder blue and embossed with cream-coloured seashells in one corner.

It began:

*Señor Callero,*

*Although this is not an easy decision to make, I feel that it is in the best interest of both myself and the Key West Ballet Theatre to discontinue my -*

He stopped before the signature. He knew who it was from.

**Pam Berg**

## Part one: Bananaphobe

*"Ladies and gentlemen, let's play some roller derby! First up jamming for the Fembots is number zero, Kaimeleon. On the line for the Nutcracker Sweets is last year's MVP, fan favourite Strawberry Jammer!"*

I hate Strawberry Jammer.

Most people retract statements like that. Hate's a strong word, they say, but she just makes me want to hit her sometimes. Well, I get to hit her all the time. I've even hit her so hard that I'm the one who bruised. The sound of the air rushing from her lungs, and the look of surprise on her face as she sails through the air, give me the same tingly rush I used to get from cigarettes. Sweet, guilty pleasure...

Also, I really do hate her.

Tonight is bout night, which means the stands are packed with screaming fans, and my head is supposed to be packed with strategies and plays. But here I am, standing on the track in the starting line-up, the whistle about to blow, and all I can think of is taking her down.

From my position as a blocker in the pack, I watch her skate out to her starting point at the jammer line. I'm shooting her a death-glare, but she won't notice. She probably doesn't see me as anything more than one of four blue-clad obstacles. She kneels down like a sprinter; bottled energy just waiting to explode. I can't see her eyes, but I know she's watching us from beneath her helmet, looking for the weak spot in our defence. Our jammer, Kaimeleon, towers over her, weight balanced on her toe-stops, the fingers of one hand clenching and unclenching. It's time.

The whistle blows, and the action surges all over the track. Everything in derby happens so fast that your thoughts come in rushes and your reactions can't wait. My team has formed a wall of blockers behind our opponents, all four of us so tight against each other that nothing gets by. Berry's darting back and forth and pushing us forward, trying to squeeze through. We're holding our ground and driving her toward the inside line, and I see a perfect chance to knock her out of bounds. As my hips sweep in and our bodies collide, all I can think is, *yes!*

Do I want to injure a fellow skater, one who happens to be my former best friend? No. But I'm thinking a few solid, bone-jarring legal hits will help me get my head back in the game.

Let's be clear: Strawberry Jammer is not my best friend. That person is trapped somewhere inside a self-absorbed megalomaniac in a purple jersey, being buried deeper every day. Ava – the name she went by before she became a minor celebrity, and the one I've known her by for the last eight years – is a total sweetheart. She loves cats and community gardening, and brings baked goods to work to brighten everyone's day. She's a terrible dancer with a dizzying knowledge of historical trivia from countless hours spent with her nose in a book. And, most importantly, she's a good friend.

Berry, Jammy, Jamcakes; these are among Strawberry Jammer's nicknames in our league, and among her fans. Oh yes, she has a following. I lost count when I un-liked her Facebook fan page, but she got popular like a cat video on the internet. It's pretty common for skaters to have fans, especially jammers. They score the points, so they're the ones in the spotlight. But she seems to have an extra shiny star over her head, and I don't mean the one on her helmet. She's one sponsorship offer away from having her own action figure.

People with fan pages were something we used to laugh about, before derby.

Before derby. We're only in our second season, and already I can barely remember what life was like without rollerskates. Ava and I bought ours after seeing a documentary at a local film festival. It appealed to us on so many levels. Female power. Athleticism. Community. Who wouldn't want some of that? I've been a bit of a jock my whole life, and skating came naturally. Plus, I was stoked to find a full-contact team sport that welcomed just about everyone, that you didn't have to have played since birth to pick up. Ava wouldn't have stood a chance otherwise.

"Watch your out!" At the sound of my pivot's voice, my hips instinctively swing toward the outside line, clipping Strawberry Jammer's offensive blocker as she tries to sneak up and distract me.

Ava had no sports background, or even basic coordination. She could injure herself walking up stairs. The first time we went out on our skates, she took two steps forward, fell off the driveway, and ate grass. But you didn't have to be a rockstar to try out, you just had to be able to skate. And after a couple of months spent practising on the streets, even Ava could do something that probably definitely passed for skating.

The night we tried out, she was terrified. If it wasn't for me she would have stayed locked in a toilet stall, afraid she was going to puke on the track, begging me to take her home. Maybe that was one of those big moments in life where there's a fork in the path. Maybe if I'd let her convince me, we'd still be friends. True, I wouldn't have experienced the exhilaration of flying around the track at top speed on nothing more than my own eight wheels. I wouldn't have felt pride in mastering new moves, or made so many new friends. Why couldn't derby just give me all of that, without turning my best friend into an asshole?

Amanda and Kai, two skaters in our Fresh Meat tryout group, haven't changed at all. Amanda is just like Ava, or how Ava used to be, anyway. She's into the environment and causes, and basically a positive person with a big heart. Kai is a six-foot tattooed lesbian with a penchant for little dogs and hideous sweaters. I've never met a more honest person, or a funnier one. We all hit it off, and used to grab beers after practice and go to Amanda's to play board games. Of course, we'd just end up talking about derby. Who we idolised, where we dreamt of skating one day. And, most importantly, what our names should be.

We spent hours agonising over our potential aliases. My alter ego is Bananaphobe. I have a lot of hang-ups, like partially closed drawers and those strings on bananas that I refuse to eat. Kai went with Kaimeleon so that people would still call her Kai. She said she couldn't handle thinking about anything except skating while she's on the track. Amanda went with Jean Grave because under her worldly exterior she's a comic book nerd.

Skaters usually don't pick names that pigeonhole them into a particular position, but there was no denying how well Strawberry Jammer fit Ava. She's small, cute, and, it'd turn out, unstoppable.

Once we got beyond the basics, our talents started to emerge. I'm a strong offensive blocker, thanks to my rugby and hockey background. Kai is a runner and naturally fast, with long legs that let her step over and through anyone in her way when she jams. Amanda kind of struggles with almost everything, but she's got a great attitude and never gives up. Ava, though... No one saw that coming.

One day she was stiff and awkward, and the next, it was like everything fell into place. She took more chances, learned new tricks. She was light on her feet and agile, able to fit through holes in the pack that no-one else spotted. I didn't understand it, since off-skates she was still a walking disaster, but I was proud. People started to notice her, and I hoped that the constant compliments would bolster her confidence. I certainly never thought they'd come between us.

Next thing we knew, it was time for the draft. The house teams got to choose skaters to fill vacancies in their rosters, and us Freshies were having daily meltdowns. Of course, we all wanted to get on the same team. But with three teams, it wasn't likely. Sure enough, Ava and Amanda went to the Nutcracker Sweets, and Kai and I got picked up by the Fembots. It was exciting and scary at the same time, like the end of high school. You know you're going on to something bigger, something you've been dreaming about, yet you can't help but wonder if you're ready.

We saw each other less as we trained for the season, and hardly at all when it started. But even though things were strained, we talked as much as we could. Ava started getting a lot of attention after games, people requesting interviews and clamouring for autographs. And then she was chosen to play for the Red Queens, the A-team that travels and competes all over the country. That was when things crashed. She stopped calling, stopped texting, and disappeared completely. What kind of person blows off her friends as soon as she becomes a big deal? I just don't get it. One thing I do know is that I don't deserve it.

And as my body collides again with hers, I just want to hit her so hard she turns back into my best friend.


## Part two: Kaimeleon


Right now, there are way too many bodies in my personal space.

I look for Bananaphobe's muscular frame, my offensive ally who's normally nearby, knocking blockers out of my way. 'Nana is skating with the defence though, because for now we're throwing all of our effort into stopping Strawberry Jammer. Smart move. That girl's slippery.

"Jammer inside! Stay on her! We've got her, we've got her!" Their pivot calls my position to her team. Not for long, I think.

I dart quickly from side to side, leading the purple blockers to follow my movements. Back and forth, baiting them. Someone will be a millisecond off and that's where I'll get through. In my peripheral, I see 'Nana sweep Strawberry Jammer out, but I don't look. Getting out of this pack is top priority. One more fake to the left and there it is, their outside blocker looking inside, not noticing her wheels are inches shy of the outside line. In a single stride I'm there. In one almost subconscious movement, I contract my entire core and inhale, make myself as small as possible and skirt sideways on my toes around her hips.

Two sharp blasts on a whistle signal that I'm the lead jammer. I accelerate into a turn, focused on the next lap and scoring points.

> "Looks like Kaimeleon is your lead jammer. There's no stopping that one,
> she's a tower of power. Strawberry Jammer is down from a huge hit
> by number four-oh-one-one Bananaphobe, but don't worry folks, she's
> given the refs the thumbs up to say she's just winded and that this jam
> is still on."

I glance over my shoulder and see Berry getting to her feet where she landed among the referees, giving a quick shake as she re-enters behind our wall to try again. She gets hit all the time; it's the nature of the beast when you're a jammer, skating around with a star-shaped target on your head. But the big hits do damage beyond bruises. They steal your speed, they steal your breath, and they put you off your game. And I'm willing to bet that one packed some extra punch.

What is it with those two? It's like dealing with the fallout from a bad breakup these days. Outside derby, I don't see what's changed. I guess some people just can't separate life from derby, that's the problem. 'Nana is sulking around with a chip on her shoulder, and Berry has gone AWOL. I don't know if it's a defence mechanism, reverse psychology, or if it's that she really has no clue that her best friend thinks she's turned into a diva. Berry is a lot of things, my constant nemesis on the track being one of them, but she's not actually a jerk. Is she?

I have my own feelings about her, not that anyone's ever asked. We both tried out for the A-team at the end of last season, and I didn't make it. I don't dwell on things; next time I try out I'll be ready. I'm lead jammer right now, after all. But we never talked about it, and that seemed weird. She wasn't my best friend or anything, but I felt like we'd become pretty close, and I kind of expected her to at least say "I'm so sorry, you deserved it" or "I wish you'd got on the team with me" or something. Anything.

There's that, and then… at the post-season Halloween party, Berry got kind of drunk. A lot of people did, I mean, it was a house party full of derby girls; it's always the same scene. Everyone starts out having a good time, then people start wrestling, and eventually the night tapers off into a few people heading to a bar to party 'til the sun comes up, and a few stragglers lurking in a kitchen telling each other way too much personal information. Berry's not a big drinker, but I never knew why until that night.

I was there with one of the league's veterans, Jet Scream. Not with her, as in, *with* her, though I wanted to be. I'd asked her to go with me and was hoping she would, I don't know, notice that we liked all the same things and that I'm incredibly witty and that maybe she was in love with me. We were having a great conversation about the bleakness of Canadian fiction when Berry came bouncing up. She started blathering on and on about this boot camp coming up in Portland and how we should all go. I tried to politely disengage with a look that meant, "I'm in the middle of something, take off!" But she didn't get it, just kept talking. And then a disco song started and suddenly they were dancing, and I was standing alone.

Well, Jet was dancing. I don't know what Berry thought she was doing, but the old Berry with zero swagger was jerking about all over that cramped living room. I tried to be cool and just wait until they were done. But they kept dancing and Berry kept chattering, and Jet didn't show any sign of coming back. Maybe she was just being polite. Or maybe it had something to do with the fact that Berry was leaning so close to be heard over the music that they were practically sharing the same air. It looked like Jet was going to get her nose taken off by one of Berry's flailing hands. They just kept getting closer, and I couldn't take it anymore.

I danced my way over and tried to casually get in the middle, yet another thing that's hard when you're the size of a small tree. Berry didn't seem to care whose attention she had, but Jet asked me what I was doing. I told her I'd thought we could go somewhere else and pick up our conversation. She looked at me with this totally blank expression, then one of realisation, then pity. She said when I'd asked her to go with me, she thought I'd meant so we didn't have to arrive alone.

The whole time she was talking to me, her eyes kept flicking back to Ava.

Un-fucking-believable. I've been rejected before, who hasn't? But to have the one girl I'd met in the last year that I thought was smart, funny, athletic, and gay blow me off for my straight, inebriated friend? What was I supposed to do with that? I knew it wouldn't amount to anything – 'Nana later told me Jet left for another party and Berry broke a lamp and got sent home in a cab – but on top of the tryouts it really stung. It wasn't her fault Jet wasn't into me, and clearly she's not my type if she went for someone dancing like Elaine from *Seinfeld*. I'm over it, and back to wondering where all the smart, funny, athletic lesbians are. We're a rare breed.

I don't know why she and 'Nana are fighting, but those two need to get their heads out of their asses. This is a sport. Just like there's no crying in baseball, there's no room for emo-baggage on the track. Right now, the only feeling I have is one of absolute elation, because I'm coming up on the pack fast, and no one sees me because they're all focused on Berry. Thanks, girl. At least this time you can't get in my way.

### Part three: Jean Grave

> *"Kaimeleon is charging up on the pack like she's on fire and – OH! What was that? She jumped through on the inside and no one even saw it coming. That's a grand slam, five points for Kaimeleon. Strawberry Jammer is still having trouble getting through the pack. It looks like her blockers are trying to make her some holes but the Fembots' defensive line is impenetrable. Let's hear it from the Kaimeleon fans in the house."*

The crowd erupts in cheers, and my voice is right in there with them. Even though I'm wearing my purple Sweets jersey over my jeans, I always cheer for my friends on both teams. That's kind of how it is with derby; you cheer for great plays or your favourite players, not just the team you like best. Heck, sometimes you even applaud a great jam by the team you're playing against. I've seen Kai high-five the opposing jammer on their way back to the bench. There's this supportive spirit that hasn't gone away, despite the slow mainstreaming of the sport. That's one of the things I like best about it. If it wasn't like that, someone like me wouldn't be here.

A wave of sadness washes over me, but I distract myself by waving the sign I painted up for Kai earlier today. I'm not going to get bogged down by the fact that, once again, I'm benched.

The captains always use a gentler expression like "non-rostered player", but any skater who didn't make the cut knows she's been benched. It's such a solid, final-sounding word. Past-tense. Done. But I'm not done. I may not have made the roster yet again, but I've got to keep trying.

The fact is, on skates I'm just abysmal. My league-mates try to help me get better, and they're always giving me encouragement and advice. I just don't get it. My limbs never have the fluidity that Kai and Berry have when they do laps, or the agility that 'Nana has all the freaking time. It's like her butt has a magnet in it, and no matter where the jammers go, she's always in their path without even turning her head. Why can't I do that? I'd give anything to just once hear the announcer comment on a fantastic hit that I did. But you have to be on the roster to get announced.

There I go, sounding bitter again. It's a constant struggle, especially on game days. I fix a smile back on my face and focus on watching the pack, making mental notes of things I should try next practice.

I know everyone has things that elude them. Skills they wish they had, things that drive them nuts. It just seems like everyone else can just work a little harder and get there. I come to every practice, bust my ass the entire time, and still have trouble doing a basic mohawk stop or timing a hit.

It was like this from day one. All through Fresh Meat, I knew I might not even make a team. Once I did, you'd think it would have been a relief. It wasn't. Instead, I'm constantly aware that I have to show The Sweets that they didn't make a mistake. I watch everyone else get better, while I continue to flounder. I try to stay positive on the outside, but deep down I have no idea why they picked me.

I've been on exactly one official bout roster in the last year, and that was because we had a bunch of girls away and injured. Even then, they only put me out a couple of times each period. I get it, but it hurt just the same. I honestly don't know which is worse, not being on the roster, or being on the bench for the entire game, and being the one whose helmet everyone pats as they sit down after a jam. Having your friends family come to watch, and then seeing them struggle to think of something nice to say afterwards...

If everyone else didn't seem to believe in me so much, I'd probably have given up ages ago.

I won't, though. I'm a great communicator, and know strategy better than most of my team from growing up watching sports with my dad. The plays make sense to me, even if I can't make my body execute them. One day I'm going to be a pivot. I'll be out there calling strategy for my blockers, and we'll make magic happen. That's the dream, and I just have to keep believing that it will come true. I'll keep signing up for boot camps and open scrimmages, and hoping for that moment when it finally clicks.

"Go Kai, go!" A young girl next to me is jumping up and down, her face made up to match Kai's trademark lizard paint. Her mother stands beside her, also cheering, both of them wearing Fembots shirts. I can't help but break into a grin.

I'm not like 'Nana; I didn't try out to find yet another sport to add to my repertoire. I tried out because I wanted to be a part of what looked like a women's movement on wheels. Discovering this hidden gem in a world of male-dominated sports was unbelievable. It combines strength, endurance, and agility. It requires quick thinking and the ability to get over mistakes quickly and learn from them one jam to the next. You really do have to give it everything you have.

Even if you're a bench-warmer, you still have this sense of ownership. We do everything ourselves, and every time I see one of our bout posters featuring my artwork taped to a billboard, I get goosebumps. It's incredibly empowering, and being a part of it means a lot to me.

> "Kaimeleon is coming around the track for another pass, will she pick up another five points? Remember folks, a jammer gets a point for every opponent that she passes including the other jammer, so right now the Sweets want to get Strawberry Jammer out of there."

I wave the sign in hopes of Kai seeing it, but she's got tunnel vision and probably only sees the track ahead. 'Nana seems hell-bent on making Berry's life miserable in that pack, which the average spectator would think is just a blocker doing her job. I know better, though.

Those two have been locked in a silent war for what feels like ages. It's sad to see such good friends have a falling out, but it's also getting kind of annoying. They have to realise how awkward it is for the rest of us, always having to change the subject if someone accidentally mentions the other. Never inviting them both to hang out. And I have to admit, part of me thinks it's just plain selfish to be fighting over something so shallow like who's a better skater or has more fans or whatever. Must be nice to have that kind of time on your hands.

Maybe it's inevitable with all these emotions and personalities, people getting rubbed the wrong way and fights flaring up. Usually it stops as quickly as it starts, but there's always gossip going around, and there are always a few bad apples saying catty things behind someone's back. Most of us don't listen and don't give a rat's ass, but when the talk turns to your friends, you get drawn in. Did she really turn into a diva when she made the travel team? Did she really sleep with that Team Canada coach to make the World Cup roster? Does she really request a bowl of green M&Ms in the locker room on game days? Okay, maybe not the last one, but the rest is just as ridiculous.

I tug on the corner of my pristine jersey and sigh. I'd give anything to be skating right now.

## Part four: Strawberry Jammer

> *"And it looks like Kaimeleon is out of the pack with more points, but Strawberry Jammer snuck through on her heels. Smart play by Strawberry, because the Fembots opened up a hole in their defence to let their own jammer through, and couldn't see her until it was too late."*

Finally. I take a few ragged breaths, willing my feet to keep moving one in front of the other and to close the gap between me and Kai. If I could just catch up, stop her from scoring any more points. But it's like my limbs know that the Fembots' defence is waiting, and don't want to get back to that pack. Why has this jam been so hard? I can't remember ever feeling so annihilated in a B-level bout. My legs feel like cement blocks, and I don't know if I have the steam to get through this lap, let alone the rest of the bout. Their blockers are on fire tonight. If I didn't know better, I'd swear 'Nana had it in for me.

If I didn't know better. That's something you say when you know it's not actually true. I'm almost certain she was out for blood in that jam, like she has been all the time lately. I don't even know why. It's not like we had a big fight and stopped being friends. One day we were inseparable, and now she won't even look at me unless she's about to hit me. Now, when I could really use a friend.

Ever since I was drafted to the Red Queens, things have been insane. At first, it was exciting. Who wouldn't be thrilled to play with the top skaters in the league? And taking a chance on a rookie, too; it was a huge honour. But it wasn't long before it became completely draining. Now that I play for two teams, I'm practising almost every night after work, not to mention weekends filled with scrimmages and bouts. I come home late all wired from skating, can't fall asleep for hours, and basically shuffle through every day like a zombie. The worst part? I'm skating so much that I'm actually too tired to be any good. I can't win.

Physical exhaustion aside, I can't remember the last time I went out and had fun. People stopped inviting me to things when they got sick of hearing "I can't, I have derby."

I haven't made any friends on the Queens yet; everyone is friendly enough at practice, but this team is so much more serious about their training, so there isn't really time for talk. They've all known each other for years, and already have all these inside jokes and have met each other's families and stuff. I'm like an awkward little kid trying to hang with the cool crowd. The last time I tried to loosen up and be social, at the Halloween party, I ended up drinking too much and probably scaring everyone away with my dancing. I'm glad I don't remember any of it.

I make sure to never complain, because there are girls in the league who'd sell their mother's kidney for my spot on the team. But sometimes I just want to lock myself in my apartment for a week and pretend that derby doesn't exist.

There was a time when skating terrified me. 'Nana had to practically force me to try anything involving physical activity, and derby seemed like a sure-fire way to break my bones and die. But I wanted to be able to say I'd done something truly adventurous, just once. Trying out was the hardest thing I've ever done, because I was sure they'd take one look at my pasty 'library tan' and see right through me to my gutless core. Yet no one told me to leave. I wasn't particularly good, but I somehow got the invite to join Fresh Meat. I felt like I'd pulled off a scam, like maybe they weren't looking all the times I tripped or flailed my arms. But every time I came to practice, there were more words of encouragement from the coaches.

I learnt to trust my gear and my body. Soon, all I wanted to do was skate all the time. I went to boot camps, joined pick-up teams, and watched derby online to study the superstars' moves. I was in love.

> "Strawberry Jammer is tearing up the track, trying to catch Kaimeleon before she can put more points on the board for the Fembots. Strawberry's sure taken a beating in this jam. That's one jammer who'll be happy when it's all over."

These days, what I feel toward my skates is more like resentment. I worked so hard to be the best skater on my team, and the result was being promoted to lowest skater on a better team and losing all my friends. I know the challenge is supposed to be the reward, but it sure doesn't feel like one. I wouldn't mind being the one struggling to keep up at practices again, if I had someone to talk to about it.

When I found out I'd made the Queens, there was a practice that night and new drafts were invited. I got the email on my way home from work, so I grabbed my gear and went straight there. I couldn't believe they'd taken me. I knew they'd never had rookies on the team before, but it never occurred to me that I was the only one. Then I got there and saw that the other new drafts were all veterans. By the time I got home, the email announcement had gone out to the league, and everyone was singing my praises for making the cut. Everyone but 'Nana, who chose that night to stop speaking to me.

I knew she was probably upset that I didn't tell her first, but that wasn't my fault. The fact that she didn't give me a chance to explain was unfair. What pride I'd felt at making the team was squashed. I pretty much gave up right then and there. I could have talked to Grave or Kai, I suppose, but I didn't want to sound like I was trying to make them take sides and I really don't deal well with confrontation. It was easier to just disappear.

What was I supposed to do? Was I supposed to quit the Queens? Should I say no to signing programmes for little girls who've finally found some positive female role models? Ignore fans, make them think we're rude and never come back? No matter what I do, I just seem to make things worse. I just want my life back. And I want this damned jam to end, because the announcer's right. I'm beat.

Four whistle blasts answer my silent prayer.

> *"Kaimeleon uses her lead jammer status to call it off before they reach the pack, stopping Strawberry Jammer from scoring. That's zero points for the Sweets in this round. But that's the beauty of roller derby, ladies and gents. Every jam's a new jam."*

I feel a hand on my shoulder and Kai skates up beside me as we return to our benches, two fresh lines already taking position.

"You okay? You kinda got rocked out there."

"I'm alright," I say, still trying to catch my breath. "But you were awesome. I can't wait 'til you're on the Queens with me."

She breaks into a lopsided grin as she veers off-path to high five Grave in the crowd on the way to her bench. I see another Fembot skating back ahead of me and before I can overthink it, I reach out and smack her butt.

"Your timing is killing me tonight."

'Nana glances over her shoulder. "I've been working on it."

"You never had to work very hard to kick my ass."

I see her chew her lip, but she says nothing.

"Think you can do it again?"

She looks at her skates for a moment, then back at me. The corners of her mouth twitch into a smile. "See you in the next jam."

**Jemima von Schindelberg**

"You're coming out with me," she'd told him. "That'll unbruise your heart."

There was no room for argument. Distraction. Diversion. Downplay the heart-break. Live a little. He'd heard it said that the best revenge was a life fully lived. There was a lot to be said for her plan. Maybe he'd get back on the horse; a horse that could reassure him he wasn't broken and forever doomed by one failure. One failure stretched over three debilitating years. Three increasingly desolate years that seemed preferable to being alone. Tonight could be the night J called to apologise for behaving like an idiot, backed down and begged forgiveness. Best be out and busy having fun or who knew where that path could lead? It was for the best that things had turned out this way. They didn't share the same goals, they couldn't be together. It was for the best. It was definitely for the best.

But did 'turning out for the best' have to hurt so much?

Engaging in a debate between agony and logic only led to more agony. Another painful truth circumstances had forced him to confront. Things had been nice, things had been horrible. He missed the loving, he was scarred by the neglect. If he'd only…if he could have just…he should've known enough to… Two weeks of analysing every conversation, gesture and silence had led to no significant insight. It hadn't brought him peace. But distraction. Distraction was worth exploring. And by the time he next looked at reality he'd be over the hurt. Simple enough plan. With any luck he could stay distracted until he was too into some-one else to care.

As they settled into a nicotine-infused seat on the second bus she mentioned that the comforting night out ahead of them was her friend's wedding.

"What?" he huffed. "Really? I get my heart smashed to pieces and you think taking me to witness the union of two lovers will make it better? Really?"

"Yes, really. It'll be a laugh."

He should have realised. Look at her! Of course. She was wearing high heels. Her talons were painted red and she'd even smoothed some shiny, sparkly goop onto her lips. And she was showing off her legs. That never happened.

"Melly!" He whined. "Mel-Mel, why? No. Can't we-? No. I thought we were head-ing to a dirty bar to dance our feet off and get shitfaced on four-for-a-fiver shots of paint-stripper, then cry noisily onto each other in the taxi home about how all men are bastards, followed by takeaway curry and beer and falling asleep with our faces on our poppadoms."

"You know I don't drink!"

"Since when?" he scoffed.

"Urgh. Don't you listen to anything I say? I have training first thing. I need to be at the peak of fitness. I can't put that rubbish inside me, I'm an athlete now."

With great willpower he hid his amusement and feigned great interest in the condensation on the window. She'd used that line once before. He remembered responding with something smart like 'on what planet are you an athlete, one with no gravity or visible light?' He'd followed this ejaculation with what could reasonably be termed a torrent of laughter. Within seconds her torso made con-tact with his and he found himself on the floor with Mel standing over him entirely unflustered.

By way of apology she simply repeated her mantra:

"I'm an athlete now."

So he'd simply learned not to laugh at her. Not out loud. He wasn't unconvinced that a barge from her now could force him right through the side of the bus.

Shouldn't little sisters stay little? He liked it better when she was small enough to tie to trees to use as target practice for his frisbee.

She clattered down side streets in her bad shoes. Shiny, red and high; defi-nitely bad. He stomped behind her on once-hip trainers. It was dark already and there was an unpleasant nip in the air. He hated this time of year. The only consolation was having a warm body to come home to; the snuggles, someone to winter with. A horrible gnawing that started with the cold biting his fingertips reminded him those days were gone. The gripping at his stomach held a threat that this cold and lonely imitation life could be his forever.

Stop thinking about it.

Something was burning, a whiff drifted towards them. The distant sound of chatter. Closer. Closer. They turned a corner into a car park packed with a human peacocks.

"FEAR!"

Thirty women and a couple of men shrieked as she gazelled towards them. Arms reached out and wrapped around her. Excitement rippled.

"Oh my God, look at you. And smell you. Gorgeous."

"I love your earrings. Razorblades, Fear, that's so funny."

"Oh my God, what did the consultant say? When can you skate?"

"Who's your date? He's so cute. Yes, I can call your brother cute. Cute. Cute Brother Fear."

"Oh my God, I thought you wouldn't make it in time for the handfasting."

The bride caught Mel's eye and gave her an excited grin. Mel winked back.

The tide of words buffeted him, unsteadied his footing. Surrounded by strange women, in an irregular gloom, he found his skin didn't quite fit. His bones itched and wriggled. If he had to come, and Melly was pretty forceful on that point, he wished he hadn't had to come alone.

Stop thinking about it. J who? Loneliness what? Focus instead on these people and their beautiful outfits. Focus on feeling like an out-of-place, under-dressed slob in a sea of normal people, elegant people. Normal people? The bride stood in the middle of a maze of fire. Her hair, even in the flickering quarter-light, was so pink it winded him. The groom, a patchwork magician of colour and texture, had skin worked with ink and metal into art.

This was the sort of outcome the family feared when Melly announced she'd taken up rollerskating and joined a wild underground cult. Firstborn's sexuality was, after a period of teeth-gnashing adjustment, tolerable, adding a trendy accent to their lives. But the baby falling into a den of nonconformity? Tattoos were a step too far. Melly's little hobby had become a subject they just didn't discuss.

It took the heat off him; when he wasn't worrying for the safety of her soul, he was quite grateful for the diversion.

Attentive eavesdropping filled him in. The happy couple were very happy. The very happy Louise and Cesar who'd had their legal ceremony earlier in the day and were now enjoying the real thing. Everyone was so very happy. This woman was so happy that the dresses had turned out so well. That woman was so happy that the couple liked the car she'd wangled for them. Another was flapping with delight about having managed to pull the catering together in such a short time with no budget. Everyone had played their part. He wondered what Melly had provided.

A feathered shaman led the couple through flames. They grinned, absorbed, fascinated, as if seeing each other for the first time. He led them to the fire, tied their hands in a comet's tail of colour and the deed was done. They kissed, friends cheered, cameras flashed, tears were wiped from under eyes, facial muscles began to cramp from smiling for so long. It was beautiful, he saw that it was beautiful, but it was so very far away. He was in a cage.

The trail of celebratory chatter led to a buffet room in a nearby building. Another favour called in from another friend. He was glad to be away from the cold and to take the weight off his feet but now there was bright light and the demand for interaction with strangers. He looked around and didn't see anyone who would take his mind off the bleeding shards of a heart now stabbing at his ribs. No, this wasn't the night he'd been looking for.

Mel removed her furry jacket and placed it on the back of an empty chair at a busy table. It was a dress not a skirt. Creamy coloured and silky to the touch, the entire back section had been embroidered with scarlet thread. A smattering of hearts and birds and flowers framing words that read 'The Mel of Fear' in delicate letters three inches high. He'd never seen her look so beautiful. Her familiar pinched suspicion was gone; her cynical eyes were wide and alight. She looked alive. She looked at home. After brief small-talk with people who had improbable verbs and abstract nouns, pop culture references and barely-veiled smut for names, she led him to a table of food.

He exhaled the 'we meet again, old friend' sigh of sad familiarity. Yeah, he was definitely going to find a life partner and make it work if he filled his arteries with cholesterol and swelled his belly with self-loathing. Cake, though. Little mountains of twinkling cupcakes. Creamy bite-size gardens blooming with colour. Labelled. Labelled beyond anything he'd seen at a party before. Gluten-free on stand one, vegan on stand two, vegan with nuts, vegan without nuts, gluten-free and vegan, egg but no dairy; supplies were depleted. And then the very-well stocked tower of 'meaty'.

"What's in those then? Bacon and lambfat?"

"Oooooh," a voice rumbled from his side, "I'd have all of those."

Someone he'd been introduced to a few minutes earlier. He didn't recall her name. In his head he'd assigned her the title 'Scary Muscles.' She was shovelling cake and meat onto a paper plate with speed and precision.

"Filthy cow-licker," Mel gave her a look.

A scarily-muscled shoulder barged at Mel in response. He cleared his throat to protest but his sister needed no defence. She didn't move, just adopted a weary expression and sighed.

"Was that it?"

"Try mine," she urged him, pointing at a clearly appreciated section. "Orange and almond. They're amazing."

Veganism. The witchy business mother feared the most. It was part of a magic that seemed to be fuelling a resurgence of confidence in Mel. They couldn't hate that, could they? She had been such a bubbly, feisty thing in her teens. But her spirit had been missing for a while. She'd started working, had that thing with that fella. Matthew was it? No, Martin, and she ended up unravelling. Sad, withdrawn and eating without pleasure or need. He cursed himself for not being more sympathetic at the time. Because he got it now. He understood. Maybe the Mel standing next to him at the buffet, who smiled and spoke up and wore her body comfortably, was a sign for him. His heart was broken because everything had gone wrong; he was hurt and broken and it wasn't fair, but that was the oldest story in the world. A well-worn story in a world that kept on keeping on. Melly had found a path out. His lungs swelled with pride and he prickled with the possibility of hope.

Pockets of the room had emptied. It had started to get quiet. Glances were exchanged between the DJ and certain guests. Having no one to talk to he noticed her absence. Where had Melly gone?

A hand slapped onto his shoulder. He turned to face a little sister tall with a steadier, fake height now. Little sister with wheels beneath her feet. He'd never been to see her skate, never cheered for her to win. This thing had become so huge for her, it scared him. Here she was, Melly the bold and brave, in an ornate white dress and rollerskates. Not what he'd expected at all.

"Today's a big day for me. I'm glad you're here, you're a brilliant big brother, and I love you. I know things have been rough but there's a lot of beauty still in the world. Try to see it. And make the most of this, because it ain't happening again."

"What--?"

"I have to go. Be happy for me."

She swooshed away in one smooth curlicue, negotiating around elderly aunts, stroppy toddlers and clustered waiters extending trays of tall-stemmed glasses to the dancefloor in the middle of the room. The bride was there too, also now on wheels. And a third be-skated woman, sober-faced and loving, with a jewelled book lying open in her hands. A ring of women in waistcoats, bowties, puffball skirts, hotpants, fishnets and evening wear rolled around them. A coven. A protective, adoring coven.

A wedding march sounded over the P.A. Wait, wasn't that the music from *Flash Gordon*? This was silly. And there was Mel, beautiful Melly, centre stage, gazing into the eyes of the bride, who was apparently now her bride. Red stitches, just like Mel's declared Lou de Change on the back of her dress. Everyone turned to look, no one laughed. Many gazed on with gentle curiosity, sharing his confusion. But no one laughed.

A steady voice focused their attention.

"For those of you who don't know me, I'm Hazey."

Knowing look.

"Well, I did have a glass of bubbly earlier."

Ripple of laughter.

"I've been very happily married to my derby wife for nearly two years now, and it's an honour to be asked to officiate at this derby wedding between my dear friends and teammates Lou and Fear and welcome them into this fine, ahem, institution. If they only get to know a tenth of the support and love that has marked my derby marriage, well, you know the rest. They'll be very blessed indeed."

She gave a discreet wave to a woman in the crowd who yelled a graceless, enthusiastic "love you, Wifey!" back at her.

Hazey set her face to professional poise, and addressed the crowd once more.

"For those of you who may not be familiar with the institution of derby marriage, I'll try to explain. It's a long standing tradition in our sport for skaters who feel that special connection to each other to formalise their bond with a ceremony and the shared title 'derby wife'. A derby wife is more than a friend, although friendship plays a crucial role, and a derby wife is different to a lover, although we love our derby wives dearly. Your derby wife is the skater you turn to when you don't make the team and want to throw in the towel. She talks you down and convinces you that forty push-ups and an hour of plank will make everything better. She is the skater you will happily remind to 'skate it out' when everything has become too much. She is the skater you watch out for, who has your back. You defend her, protect her and when necessary slap her back into place if she's got too big for her boots. She is the missing piece in your puzzle."

Heads nodded. Hands reached for hands.

"It's traditional for derby wives to be wed by Elvis himself, but this isn't Las Vegas and we're not at Rollercon, so you'll have to put up with me."

A reverent chuckle passed through the room.

"If anybody present has any objection to the union of these two skaters speak now and face the beating of your life." She glanced around the room. "Or hold your peace, though knowing derby girls that might be asking for the impossible."

The twinkle left her eye and her voice softened. No, this really wasn't any kind of a joke. The repeat-after-me began with just as much adoring absorption between the skater-wives as the husband-wife had shown each other an hour before.

"I take you to be my derby wife."

"I vow to always take pictures up your skirt at after-parties and to hold your hair back when you're being sick in a bin."

"I will always be your first phone call from jail, even if I was the one who got you there in the first place."

"Don't worry Mummy, we're both very law abiding citizens!" Lou called to the congregation.

Hazey continued, getting quieter, keeping the crowd's attention with no effort.

"I promise to be your biggest fan unless you're on the opposing team in a bout, then I promise to hit you harder than anyone else on the team, because I'd never insult you by going easy."

They repeated the final vow and giggled like spies.

Hazey's face broke into a massive smile.

"I now pronounce you derby wife and derby wife. You may kiss your bride."

Lips pecked and the brides whirled in a swooping hug. Standing at the side, eyes glued from a respectful distance was the groom. Clapping erupted, an explosion of happy hands led by the groom's.

"I can't believe I've had the perfect wedding twice in one day," Lou exclaimed with tears flowing freely. "This is the most amazing day of my life and you're all here with us."

She dissolved into happy incoherence.

"Thank you everybody. Love you all." Mel squawked, starting to well up.

He saw his little sister alive in a glow he couldn't possibly provide for her. A glow he couldn't really know, but he knew he had to let this be. And her bride was glowing. And her bride's husband was glowing too. So this was love? Brides and groom circling round the room separately, connected so securely they could let each other go.

Fifteen days had passed since J sat him down and said 'I love you but I can't be in a relationship with you.' Fifteen days since J laid down the options that he'd had to walk away from. Alone in the crowd, heated by dancers and drinkers, skaters and a pair of women duelling with someone's crutches. Alone in the cloud of loving independence and community. 'This is how it had to be' started to make sense.

"Are you having an okay time, Philly?"

He gave a confident nod. He got it now.

No, he didn't love enough to share, but maybe he could love enough to let go.

For a moment he flew.

**Tom Snowdon**

The dark green Mini Cooper skidded to a halt on the wet forecourt, spraying a handful of gravel onto the side of the building. A man stepped out and skipped across the car park, soles crunching on the ground. Raindrops bounced off his slick hair, onto his slick suit and down to the gleaming patent leather of his shoes. Huddled in the doorway of the building, two women in sportswear and waterproofs shared an undersized umbrella, their bikes propped against the wall.

"Hi, ladies, I'm Jake Green," he flashed them a well-rehearsed smile and offered his hand, "from Thockstons Commercial." The shorter of the two women reached out and took it. His impossibly smooth skin left a faint, cloying sweetness of aftershave behind, a colossal steel watch flapping about as they shook hands.

"I'm Hannah, that's Nell" she said. Her companion nodded and raised the pannier she was holding in greeting.

"Well, ladies, let's head inside" he jangled the keys at them, then opened the door. Behind his back Nell rolled her eyes at Hannah.

The door creaked open and the three of them stepped into the warehouse. The air was thick and musty, a dull drumming of rain on metal overhead and a steady dripping sound nearby. The estate agent flicked a switch. One by one, pale, washed-out strip lights plunked into life above. The space in front of them was clean and empty, the flat concrete floor covered with a thin layer of dust. Two pillars in the centre of the room reached up to the ceiling, their edges chipped, showing glimpses of the steel reinforcement inside. Nell strode out into the middle of the room, dropped her bag and pulled out a tape measure. She set about measuring distances; from pillar to pillar and across the length and breadth of the room. The estate agent shot his cuffs a fraction, then turned to Hannah.

"So, as we discussed, it's available immediately, with the deposit naturally, but I'd want to have a word with the current owner. Just to make sure they get these leaks fixed, and that all the paperwork's up to date. They've had it on the market for a while now so hopefully they should…"

But Hannah had already stopped paying attention to his continued sales pitch, instead casting her eyes around and wandering over to a small row of offices along one wall. She shot a glance over to Nell who was heading back towards them. Nell gave a thumbs-up and pleasantly surprised nod as she walked over. The estate agent had finished his patter and turned to the pair, expectant.

"Yup. No problem." said Nell to Hannah. "You could probably get a whole track between them if you wanted, but I reckon you'd be better putting that pillar in the middle," she gestured towards the closer of the two main supports, "then you could have folks at the end and along one side." She nodded again and turned to the estate agent. "Do you mind if I skate?"

"I er, no, er… no, I don't think so." he answered, bemused. Nell nodded, sat down, and begun to pull her kit out of her bag.

Hannah and the estate agent wandered along the row of offices along the side of the warehouse. Hannah gazed through, looking at the drab brown patchwork of carpet squares in each of the cubicles. Slivers of light punched through the dust coating the narrow, high windows on the side wall, throwing hazy grey light over the rooms. Jake was still spouting an assortment of hastily memorised facts about the location and the surrounding area. He may have had all the charm of wilted spinach, but he'd done his homework and was clearly desperate to tell someone. He turned to Hannah as she peered through another grubby window into another office, and stopped mid-flow.

"You said you were looking for a training venue, right? You know you'll have to talk to the council about the zoning and changing the building purpose?"

"Yup, we're already doing it. The council has seemed pretty responsive about it. They've agreed in principle, but it depends on the location. There's even been talk of a grant, sports development and all that, so we just need to find the right place. We've been searching for a while, but everything's been too small, too far, too run-down or just too damn expensive."

"So, what are you training for?" he asked. Nell had finished tying her laces and was on her feet, lazily skating towards the centre of the room, still checking the velcro on her elbow pads.

"Roller derby," said Hannah.

"Right. Sounds cool," he said, nodding and furrowing his brow with practised interest. "So... what's a roller derby?"

"It's a sport. Full contact. On rollerskates." She pulled her messenger bag round from her back and rummaged in the front pocket. "Here, take a flyer," she said, handing him one. "There's a bout in a couple of weeks. Come along."

"Well, er, yeah. Might do. Sounds... interesting." He slipped the piece of paper into his folder and resumed his sales pitch as they started back towards the entrance.

Nell was gently circling in the centre of the hall, one headphone in her ear, nodding gently in time to the music. The floor was smooth, crack-free, and better than she'd expected. She weaved from side to side slightly as she skated round, surveying the ground nearby. The place seemed almost too good. Decent surface, enough space for the track, room for a whole herd of zebras round the outside, and still enough left to play around with. They could run a barrier along the wall by the entrance and get some merch stands in there, maybe even a stage at the other end, if they could get bands in. That'd mean there would still be plenty of room for seating. She could see it now; a couple of decent bleacher-style arrangements, with enough room for a few hundred people, and still room in front for the nosebleed seats.

She circled the pillar at the far end of the hall in a long lazy arc, picking up a little speed again as she pushed into the straight. She glanced over at the offices; Hannah was clearly investigating while the estate agent gesticulated around the building.

She could almost hear the atmosphere building as the skaters emerged from the converted offices. The two teams skated to the dugouts opposite the audience and huddled together for their team talks. In the background the house band were tearing through their last song. The singer, a tattooed punkabilly in a leopard-print pencil dress and skyscraper heels spat and screamed her way through the song as a motley collection of jeerleaders arranged themselves into precarious human pyramids in front of the stage. A cheer went up as the band finished in a flurry of drums and squealing harmonics.

Background music faded up and the announcers' voices rang out, as the crowd shuffled back to their seats, drinks in hand. Moments later, the away team skated out. The audience applauded politely as they skated round, each of the girls saluting as the announcers called out their name. Another polite round of applause, then they made their way back to their box. There was a lull for a moment, heavy with anticipation. Then the home team stood up and started towards the track. A familiar song intro thumped out across the hall and the crowd exploded; shouting, clapping, and waving banners. High above, the corrugated metal roof rattled and echoed in response. Nell waited, balanced on her toe-stops, running through the names in her head, counting down to her own.

"Number 667! Hell's Nell!" cried the voice. Nell sprinted forward, grinning and punching the air in time with the music.

From the edge of the room the estate agent watched puzzled as the figure in the middle-distance looped back towards them, still smiling, hand held high.

Nell felt a little twinge of adrenaline as she stepped up to a join in the concrete where the jam line would be. She could imagine the freshly-marked lines, still with a matte shine where rubber wheels had yet to leave their mark. There would be no more official time-outs for NSOs to frantically re-tape the track here.

There was another momentary dip in the crowd noise before the whistles blew. Nell started at a run, high on her toes, weaving and jumping through the imaginary wall. She could hear the mouthguard-muffled shouts behind her as she broke away from the pack, crouching low and pumping her outside arm in time with her crossovers. To the left, a ref blew his whistle, raised a fist and pointed; she was lead jammer. Nell glanced back for moment, checking her opponent's progress. The other jammer had run straight into their star blocker and, much to the crowd's delight, was sprawled on the floor, frantically trying to pull her arms and legs in.

Nell turned back and leant into the oncoming turn. She raised her stance slightly heading back into the straight, looking for holes in the throng of bodies in front of her. The opposing team's jammer was still stuck on her first pass, wriggling against a solid four-wall, furiously trying to push her way through. Nell focused her attention on the opposing team's pivot. She had dropped to the back of the pack and was watching her approach as the gap between them closed. Nell shifted her hips gently from side to side and weighed up her options. She'd been lucky on her first pass, but this time they were waiting, and it wouldn't be so easy. The gap between them had closed and she pushed up against the pivot, the pair of them tight to the inside line of the track. The pivot leant back into her and two blockers appeared to her right, hemming her in to the side of the track, throwing small shoulder hits, trying to jostle her out of bounds. Nell swayed with each hit and threw her own weight back against the blocker. She pushed against the pivot trying to feel for any weakness in her defence.

They were almost at the end of the straight, and the opposing jammer had broken through and was starting to make up ground, ref flapping furiously by her side. Nell took a sharp breath and faked her body to the right. The pivot bought it, moving over to try and stop her. It was all she needed. Nell twisted her left foot a fraction and kicked off her toe-stop. There was a shout from behind as one of the opposing blockers saw what was happening, but it was too late. Nell was already in the air and over the apex. Whoops and cheers went up from the crowd as she landed on her other foot, wheeling her arms slightly to keep balance. On the other side of the track, the opposing jammer was drawing closer and closer to the back of the pack. Nell hit her hips and the jam was over, the crowd yelling their appreciation.

Nell spun her body around and jammed her toe-stops against the floor, front wheels screeching against the concrete as she came to a halt. She reached up and popped the headphones from her ears, then loosened her helmet and rolled back towards her bag. The rain had died down. The cavernous hall was almost completely silent. At the edge of the room, Hannah was taking pictures of the warehouse from every possible angle. The estate agent trotted over as Nell unlaced her skates.

"That was pretty impressive!" He had the familiar confused enthusiasm of a person who got roller derby when they were expecting roller disco. "Was the jumping bit part of it? Your friend said it was full contact? Do you go that fast when you're up against other teams? Do you actually hit people?" His salesman veneer had dropped, and a glimmer of real interest was showing through. He almost sounded genuine.

"You should come to a bout. That'll make more sense than me trying to explain it now. I think Hannah's got some flyers on her," she indicated towards her friend "all the details are on there."

"She's already given me one, thanks." He fished inside the folder and brought it out, this time turning it over and giving it more than a cursory inspection. "I'll try and come along." His mobile rang, and he excused himself, slipping back into his sales voice as he answered. He wandered away as Hannah approached.

"So...?" she said, "what do you reckon?"

Nell glanced around the room.

"It's pretty good. In fact, it's very good. Easily the best I've seen."

"Same here, and I've been to a lot," nodded Hannah, almost bouncing with excitement. "And we can afford it! There's even spare space, so we can think of doing other stuff. Can you imagine it, a real roller derby venue? Ours? Some of the other directors are already talking about renting out to other leagues as well. "

"Well, we've still got to make sure it happens. Something about counting chickens?"

"Sure. But we'll make it happen. We always make it happen."

"Well, in that case," said Nell, packing her pads back into her bag, "it's ours. Welcome home."

# GLOSSARY

**Blocker**
Up to three blockers skate in each jam, playing a combination
of offence and defence. Their job is to block the opposing
team's jammer while assisting their own through the pack.

**Brat**
Underage skater in a junior roller derby league.

**Fresh Meat**
New roller derby recruits, ones who haven't yet passed their minimum skills.

**Jammer**
The point-scoring skater, identified by the star on their helmet cover.
The first jammer to make it through the pack legally becomes lead
jammer, giving them the power to 'call off the jam' before the two-
minute scoring period ends by placing their hands on their hips.

**Minimum skills**
A skills assessment roller derby players have to pass before
they can skate in their first inter-league competition.

**Pivot**
Identified by the stripe on their helmet cover, pivots control the
speed of the pack and direct the blockers skating in that jam.

**Scrimmage**
An informal game, usually part of a league's training programme.

**Zebra**
Another name for a roller derby referee, based on their
black-and-white uniforms.

**MVP**    Most valued player

**NSO**    Non-skating official

**WFTDA**  Women's Flat Track Derby Association

# FOR BOOKS' SAKE

Founded in 2010, *For Books' Sake* is the UK webzine dedicated to promoting and celebrating writing by women, providing a dedicated platform for readers and writers alike.

With daily news, reviews, essays, features and interviews, For Books' Sake shines spotlights on classic and contemporary writing by both iconic and up-coming women authors, alongside a national live events programme involving arts and literature festivals across the UK, panel discussions, workshops and much more.

Their first publishing project was *Short Stack,* a collection of the best new pulp fiction written by women, published by and in collaboration with Pulp Press in 2012.

www.forbookssake.net / @forbookssake

# LONDON ROLLERGIRLS

What's roller derby?

"One of Britain's fastest-growing grassroots sports... the perfect pastime for feminists with attitude" *The Guardian*

"Rapidly becoming the next big thing" *The Independent*

"The most exciting sport on wheels" *Time Out*

The London Rollergirls formed in April 2006 to bring roller derby to the UK, with four league teams (Suffra Jets, Ultraviolent Femmes, Steam Rollers and Harbour Grudges), and an all-star travel team (London Brawling) and an all-star reserves team (Brawl Saints) that play teams from other cities around the world. In September 2011, London Brawling made history as the first team outside North America to take part in the WFTDA East Region Playoffs held in Baltimore, USA.

www.londonrollergirls.com / @ldnrollergirls

# ABOUT THE AUTHORS

**Pamela Berg,** aka #321 Tiki TimeBomb, is a Fresh Meat coach, captain and jammer for the Terminal City Rollergirls' Faster Pussycats. This lucky Canadian has played derby from Alaska to Australia, but spends most of her time lurking at a desk in IT. She loves snacks, cats, and wearing as much neon as possible.

**Daphne Du Gorier** is a Muslim roller-girl maniac. She's sort of funny. When she's not skating or blogging, she's asking people if they've read her latest blog about skating.

**Robyn Frame** is a secretary from Newcastle. When not skating with the Newcastle Roller Girls, she's usually drinking tea or getting up to mischief with her girlfriend and partner-in-crime, Ella. She loves music, hates cheese, and her favourite colour is rainbow.

**Kylie Grant** is a novelist and short fiction writer based in London. She currently works as a library assistant at The London School of Hygiene & Tropical Medicine, where she often has trouble spelling the names of diseases and, in fact, the word disease.

**Kat M. Gray** is a writer and teacher of writing in the Chattahoochee Valley area of Alabama/Georgia. Kat found roller derby in 2007 and began skating with the Burn City Rollers as Mary Helley #1818. She is currently beginning her fourth season, and has now changed her name to Manticora #66. Manticora idolises many fearless blockers, but most of all, the ones who have to fight through impossible odds to become the track-monsters they are.

**Gavin Inglis** incorporates hypertext, photography and music into his published fiction and spoken word performances. He recently discovered the joy of constructing fake head wounds from liquid latex.

**Evangeline Jennings** tells lies for fun and profit. Possibly born in Liverpool, her mother may have been a third generation American Beauty Queen which would make Evangeline both Southern Belle and Northern Scum. The founding editor of the Pankhearst collective, Evangeline is soon to publish an anthology of themed short stories and novellas entitled *Cars & Girls*. As a longtime fan of the TXRD Lonestar Rollergirls, Evangeline's favourite skater was, is, and will always be Chola #68. Puta por vida. No lie.

**Magda Knight** is the founder and owner of Mookychick, an online feminist hub for alternative women. She writes speculative fiction for assorted children, adults and changelings. She discusses writing and feminism in equal measure at her website.

**Steven LaFond** is a writer living in Arlington, Massachusetts with his wife, Jessie. He received his MFA from the Bennington Writing Seminars. When not writing, he announces roller derby throughout North America (with a planned 2013 stop in the UK) under the name Pelvis Costello.

**Cariad Martin** is a Kent-based writer currently seeking representation for her novel about raucous teenage girls. She has appeared on local radio and various feminist webzines talking about social issues, and is a fierce defender of the welfare system and advocate for better sex and relationship education.

**Elena Morris** is a graduate from Brighton, UK. When she's not writing, hitting girls on skates or watching *Buffy the Vampire Slayer,* she's pursuing a career that lets her work with both literature and teenagers. This is her first publication.

**Jemima von Schindelberg** is co-creator of graphic heroine Ethel Sparrowhawk and might have finished writing the next instalment if she didn't spend so much time rolling around shouting at naughty skaters. She likes whistles, trains and vegan cake.

**Tom Snowdon** is a roller derby enthusiast, semi-professional shouter and occasional writer. He lives in London with a tiny dinosaur who keeps eating all his food and telling him to stop buying guitars.

**Kaite Welsh** is an author, freelance journalist and failed rollergirl. She hoped that writing about roller derby instead of doing it would result in fewer injuries. Sadly, due to a combination of a rickety desk chair, a heavy cat and a large mug of tea, this has not proved to be the case.